The Dastardly Mr. Deeds

The Gumboot & Gumshoe Series: Book Two

Laura Hesse

Running L Productions

ISBN Print 13 digit: 978-0987734396
ASIN Amazon: B07PQ9JSCB
Cover Artist: Autumn Sky, Self Pub Book Covers Inc. Publisher: Running L. Productions, Vancouver Island, British Columbia Distributor: Amazon Worldwide

Introduction

Gumboots, Gumshoes and Murder is the first book in *The Gumboot and Gumshoe Series*. The unlikely trio of Sgt. Betty Bruce, Gertrude, and Peaches were just too delicious to ignore and appear in the sequels, *The Dastardly Mr. Deeds, Murder Most Fowl, Gertrude & The Sorcerer's Gold*, and *Chasing Santa*.

The novel, *The Dastardly Mr. Deeds*, is inspired by the real-life events surrounding the appearance of feet in sneakers on various islands up and down the British Columbia coastline and Puget Sound. The Tiffany Hyde-White's character, Mr. Deeds, is also based on real events. I am not going to tell you which part as that would spoil the story. There is an information page with links at the end of this book but don't read it until after you have finished the novel.

The Town of Lund is a wonderful little place, but there is no Angel's Heavenly Gate Funeral Home.

The character of Gertrude, the pot-bellied pig, is based on Alfie, a charming fellow who would do anything for a Milk Bone.

Seal Island is loosely based on Lasqueti Island, located between Vancouver Island and the mainland of British Columbia. It is only accessible by ferry, boat or boat plane.

Contents

"There is more in you of good than you know, child of the kindly West. Some courage and some wisdom, blended in measure. If more of us valued food and cheer and song above hoarded gold, it would be a merrier world."

J.R.R. Tolkien, The Hobbit or There and Back Again

Prelude

Gertrude and Peaches ran amuck, trampling flowerbeds and scattering Morris Tweedsmuir's goats to the four winds once again. On a whim, the pot-bellied pig and the Jersey cow raced across the boardwalk that joined the grocery store, hardware store, and the Bristling Boar Pub together. People scrambled out of their way.

Someone left the pub's door open, and the duo barged in.

An athletic and striking grey haired man with a twinkle in his eye and the red nose of an alcoholic sat at the bar. He laughed and turned his attention from the regal blond woman with the perfect smile, perfect complexion, and the luxuriously long hair, sitting beside him, to the bristling snout of the wayward pig that had placed a large head in his lap and stared longingly up at his beer. He offered the baleful eyed pig the rest of his beer.

"Oh, Barnabas, really," Camille exclaimed.

"What? It's good for her," he said indignantly.

"You are incorrigible," she sighed.

"S'okay, so is Gertie," he chimed, patting the pig on the forehead. "We're two peas in a pod, aren't we, doll?"

The pig grunted.

Camille choked on her wine.

Barney gently patted his wife on the back, a sly grin on his face.

"Don't worry, darling, I only have eyes for you," he murmured into her ear as the pig snuffled the empty beer mug in his hand.

Camille laughed, the laugh lines around her eyes deepening.

"Remember that the next time you unzip your fly," she crooned back.

"Ouch," he responded, leaning back in his chair.

The pig continued to lick the empty beer glass.

Gwen Mann raced around the bar, her mouth a thin angry line, her dark brown eyes blazing. She swatted the grey and white pig in the bum with a straw broom. Gertrude squealed in fear. Peaches bawled, the cow's feelings positively hurt by the expletives that came out of the tiny Malaysian woman's mouth as she smacked the Jersey cow's bottom with an open hand.

The men in the pub cheered raucously.

Eighty-year-old Archie Bruce stood on the pub steps, beer in hand, amused, as the pig and cow skidded by him. It was his fifth beer. He knew he should stop, but the pain in his fractured ribs hadn't disappeared until the end of the fourth mug of pale ale. Now, he was pain free and pleasantly buzzed. The only thing that hadn't dulled was the ache in his heart.

In their hasty retreat, the unstoppable pig and its sidekick bovine knocked over trash bins and broke down the porch railing on the outside deck before leaping down the last two steps to safety.

It was just another day on Seal Island.

As he ran a hand through his head of thick silver hair, Archie thanked his lucky stars that he was alive to see it given recent events on the island. Loves were lost, new loves formed, and then those too were lost. It was time to enjoy the simple things in life once again and watching his rotund pot-bellied pig and her Jersey cow cohort wreak destruction wherever they went cheered him up. The pig and Jersey cow were his problems now since he had adopted Peaches after her owner, Andy McDowell, had died in a most spectacular fall after trying to kill him, his daughter, and Violet Bone.

A stab of pain shot through his heart. He missed Vi, but he missed her deceased sister, Eliza, even more.

It was funny, he thought to himself. The yearning that churned like bittersweet chocolate deep within his soul was not for his deceased wife of fifty years, but for his best friend's wife. Eliza had been an amazing cook, an even better friend, and a wonderful writer of very bad poetry. Neither Eliza nor Archie had ever been unfaithful to their spouses, but when first Mary and then Wally had died, they discovered something amazing… they could love again.

Archie saw his daughter, Betty, standing in the cemetery at the top of the hill, the church steeple rising above her like a shining white beacon of light against the darkening rain clouds above it, looking his way. He raised his mug to her.

***

Betty waved to her father. She saw Gertrude and Peaches hightail for the docks after being chased out of the pub by Gwen Mann. She found comfort because on Seal Island, no matter the tragedy, some things never changed, and that was when her cell phone began to ring!

Betty looked at the cell phone's display. Doc Forester's name flashed across the screen. She sighed wearily. Now what?

"Hello," she answered, annoyed. She had asked the detachment commander to cut her some slack, at least for a day or two.

The raven that had been watching her lay flowers on the graves of her old friend, Eliza Bone, and her handsome beau, slash torrid romance writer, slash serial killer, Andy McDowell, returned, as if out of nowhere. It settled upon Eliza's headstone, its golden eyes meeting Betty's own. A large black wing feather fluttered to the ground.

She listened to Doc Forester's gentle voice, his words penetrating her heart.

"What do you mean, it wasn't Andy's child," whispered Betty into the phone.

Betty's hands trembled as Andy's last words, his uncharacteristic rage, and the beseeching look in his eyes as he tumbled over the cliff, flashed through her mind.

"So, what you're saying is that Andy's confession wasn't a confession at all."

***

Barnabas Whyte wandered out of the pub. He stopped beside Archie.

"You've got your hands full with those two, Archie," Barney joked with his best friend and poker buddy.

"Not really," Archie responded, "I just let them do whatever they want."

"And pay for the damages," Barney asked him.

"Pretty much," Archie agreed.

The two men laughed.

Barney noticed Betty pacing back and forth in the cemetery, talking on her phone. She was clearly agitated. His brow furrowed in thought.

"See you later, Arch," Barney mumbled, gripping the railing to keep from tumbling down the steps.

"Wife's not going with you," Archie asked.

"Cam's waiting for my pilot to get here with the float plane. Going to go do what all wives do best," the old man grumbled.

"Wreak havoc on the credit card?"

"Pretty much," Barney agreed, mimicking Archie.

"Why don't you come over for dinner then? I'll give Reggie and Stew a call. Maybe we can organize a game tonight."

"Thanks, but I've got a fresh batch of brew that wants bottling."

"You know that stuff's either going to kill you or blind you one day."

"That's the idea," Barney answered, tugging his hoodie up and over his head.

He lifted a hand in farewell before zig-zagging his way across the parking lot towards North Shore Road and the long walk home.

Archie chuckled as he watched his friend go and then polished off his beer.

And So It Begins

Gertrude's mood was as bleak as the grey day that surrounded her, having been thwarted by the pub owner's wife. What was a pig to do without a pint in the afternoon? She preferred dark ale over Guinness, but draft would do in a pinch.

The pot-bellied pig slowed to a walk. She ambled across the dock, her hooves clickity-clacking on the wooden planks. She stopped at her friend Reggie's boat. He was always good for a beer. Her friend, Peaches, waited at the landing, not liking the feel of the rolling dock beneath her feet. Gertrude didn't mind as she preferred not to share her beer.

Crab traps bounced and rattled on deck as the rising tide slapped against the rusting trawlers.

Gertrude looked up, chin whiskers quivering. There was no movement on the bridge of Reggie's boat. She sniffed. Rotting fish, pungent diesel fumes, and tar assaulted her senses.

She squealed, a high-pitched sound that hurt the ears.

No response.

Reggie definitely wasn't home.

The pot-bellied pig, hair bristling, tummy brushing the ground, trotted back down the dock and returned to the landing where the cow waited patiently. She nuzzled the cow's soft velvety nose. The cow nuzzled her back.

Not given to long bouts of self-pity, the pot-bellied pig spun on her heels, the cow a cream-colored caboose tagging along behind her.

Gertrude turned down the narrow path that led to the shore. Tall cedar and fir trees lined the winding trail. It ended on a long stretch of desolate beach.

Gertrude's mood sky-rocketed when she saw the man that she had been looking for sitting on a log a couple hundred yards away from the trailhead. She made a beeline straight for him.

***

The beach was rocky. Piles of seaweed lined the many downed logs that littered the shore below the cliffs that grew in height along the northernmost stretch of the crescent of beach. On one of these logs sat Reggie Phoenix, semi-retired fisherman and pot grower extraordinaire.

Reggie quietly nursed a can of beer, an open twelve pack of Molson Ale at his feet. His brows were knitted together beneath his warm woolen toque, an unruly crop of curly grey hair poking out from beneath it, the puzzled expression on his face making him look even older than his fifty-five years. Four days of stubble as thick as porcupine quills covered his cheeks and chin. He tugged the hem down on his grey knitted cardigan, mulling over what to do about his current dilemma.

A barrel-chested, broad shouldered man with hands like catcher's mitts, a large beer belly, and salt and pepper hair, wandered up the beach. He absently picked up a rock and threw it into the surf. It landed with a hollow 'plop' in the salt water.

"Hey, Reggie, what ya doing," Stew asked the befuddled man sitting on the log.

"Well, Stew, I was enjoying sitting 'ere on this 'ere log, just having a brewskie when that there woman done showed up," the grizzled old fisherman said, his voice as weathered as his face and hands.

"What woman," Stew asked, shooing the pig and cow away.

"That one," Reggie said, pointing at the body in the surf. Reggie squashed up the empty can of beer and stuffed it down beside the log. He then pulled another can of beer out of the box and offered the box to Stew, completely ignoring the pig who stared at him with longing in her eyes.

"Oh, that one," Stew said, reaching for a beer.

Stew popped open the can of Molson and sat down on the log beside Reggie. Both of them quietly contemplated the body.

Tiny crabs scuttled about inside the woman's dark brown hair. Her eyes were open, glazed over in death. Her skin was a pasty white. She wore a pretty pink blouse, purposely faded designer blue jeans, and sparkling white tennis shoes. One of the biggest diamond's the men had ever seen graced the ring finger on her left hand.

"She's pretty," Stew commented.

"She is so," Reggie agreed.

"Barney's wife would go gaga over that rock," Stew added. "Mine too."

Reggie nodded in agreement.

The men pondered on that for a bit.

"Ya think we should pull her out of the surf," Reggie asked Stew after a time.

"Dunno, Reg. Might be we'd disturb evidence if we do that. You know, leave our fingerprints on something we shouldn't like on that CSI program on TV."

"That's what I was thinking, Stew."

"Tide's coming in," Stew commented dryly.

The water was about eight feet away from where the men sat on the log; it crept towards their feet.

"Aye, I figure we got about a half hour before it comes all the way in and then goes out again," Reggie mumbled, his brow still furrowed, his grey eyes bloodshot. He took a swig of beer.

Stew grunted before downing his beer in one long swallow.

Behind the two men, the pig and cow nosed through the seaweed, gobbling down things of interest.

***

Gertrude had given up on anyone sharing their beer with her. No matter how many times she nosed her friend, he wouldn't offer her any.

Her tummy grumbled.

She supposed that if she searched long enough, she'd find something of interest in the seaweed. She usually did.

The tang of the salt assaulted her nostrils as she rifled through the seaweed and clam shells.

Her nose quivered. The object in front of her was red and white. It smelled delightful. She used her snout to brush the seaweed off and picked it up.

Before one of the men had a chance to take it from her, she raced past them, her prize in her mouth. It was hers!

***

"Is that a sneaker in Gert's mouth," Stew asked Reggie as the pig raced by.

"Yep, appears so," Reggie agreed, switching his attention from the body in the surf to the running pig.

"Is that a foot bone protruding out of it, Reggie?"

"Sure looks like it, Stew."

They glanced at each other over top of their cans of beer. It was proving to be both an interesting and annoying type of day.

"I suppose we better give Betty a call," Stew sighed, tossing the empty beer can atop the others lying behind the log.

"Yah, I suppose so," Reggie agreed.

***

Betty fought to control the dizzying wave of depression that threatened to overwhelm her as she closed the cemetery gate behind her and started walking up North Shore Road towards home. She didn't relish the thought of entering Andy McDowell's house and going through his things. Her conversation with the coroner had been more than a little upsetting.

She had thought the deaths of her friend, Eliza Bone, who had drowned in her fish tank, and Tiffany Hyde-White, who had died by consuming peanut laced chocolates, coupled with the tragic death of Summer River in the arms of her stone angel, had all been clever killings committed by the man she had fallen in love with. Andy's surprising confession and subsequent attempt to kill her, her father, and Violet Bone, had left her stunned and consumed with grief. Now, it appeared that he may have been innocent after all. If so, what had compelled him to lie? And why had he attacked Violet to begin with? The whole thing was as bizarre as the three women's deaths.

Betty's head was spinning, her mind reeling from the implications in the Coroner's Report. A migraine tugged at her temples, the blistering wave of pain snaking around the back of her head and up through her forehead with increasing force.

Her father intercepted Betty.

"Penny for your thoughts, Angel," Archie said to his daughter, falling in step beside her.

"Not now, Dad," she said, her words sharp and cutting. She winced. "Sorry, Pops. My head's pounding."

"Come on, get the load off," he urged her, wincing as he wrapped one arm under his daughter's. He was still suffering from the beating he had taken at the hands of Andy McDowell. The beer took the edge off for a little while, but the effects of the alcohol were already wearing off.

Father and daughter walked like that for some time, seeking comfort, the weight of the world eased by their powerful family bond.

Archie knew his daughter would open up about what was bothering her once she was ready.

The road ahead branched into two, one branch lead south-east towards the other side of the island, while the branch they were on travelled north and then north-east along the coast. Watch Tower Mountain gazed down upon them, its top shrouded by low-hanging clouds.

A herd of wild sheep grazed along the side of the road. They scattered when the pair approached them.

The "Bone's Bailiwick" sign at the end of Eliza's driveway reminded them both of their loss. A red and white 'For Sale' sign had recently been erected beside it.

Betty stopped.

"What's this?"

"Vi said she was selling the place," Archie sniffed, taking a hanky from his pocket. "She said the sign was going up tomorrow, not today."

"The Realtor sure didn't waste any time," Betty mumbled, her heart aching.

"It won't be the same without a Bone on the island," Archie grumbled, his shoulders slumping forward.

Betty hugged her father. He clasped her. She could feel the trembling in his body. She pulled away, but he held fast, not wanting to let go.

"So what's up with the phone call in the cemetery," Archie asked, finally stepping backwards. He wiped the smattering of tears from his face with a shredded hanky. He was done with being too proud to cry.

Betty didn't answer. She wandered off, her father falling into step beside her once again. She wondered how much she should tell him. Nothing, probably, but she needed a sounding board and if she couldn't trust her father, who could she trust?

"Turns out that Summer's unborn baby wasn't Andy's."

"Say what," Archie gasped.

"Yep, not his. I'm happy about that as I just couldn't see it, but it's a puzzle. Apparently, Andy's blood was full of lead and his brain showed signs of degeneration too."

"What does all that mean," Archie asked his daughter.

"Lead poisoning can cause delusions, aggression, agitation, and a whole host of other issues." Betty halted.

That was it!

That was the answer she was looking for: Andy must have been suffering from hallucinations.

"It means that we can't believe Andy's confession. Doc Forester said the degeneration was severe, and it surprised him that I hadn't noticed any odd behavior or aggression prior to this."

"So even though he confessed to killing Eliza, Tiffany and Summer, he might not have killed them," Archie gasped.

"That's right," Betty agreed. "The murders may have all been in *his* mind. At least until proven otherwise, we're back to square one and Doc Forester is sticking to his rulings of accidental deaths. The one thing that Doc Forester wants found though is the sources of Andy's lead poisoning and the LSD in his system. Doc says that the LSD was really potent, not your average back yard hodgepodge."

Archie and Betty walked on, each of them lost in their own thoughts.

"What's our next step, Angel puss," Archie asked, turning to face his daughter.

"There is no 'our next step', Dad. I, and I do mean I, am going to take a look around Andy's house to see if I can find something that might give us a clue as to what caused the lead poisoning before Doc Forester and his forensic crew get here. As for the LSD, I'm at a loss as to where to look and am quite flabbergasted."

"You know Andy had the whole house gutted a year or so ago. It was right before your mother died. Maybe it was lead in the pipes or in the paint? That house of Marilyn's is old," Archie suggested. "It was one of the first homesteads ever built on this island."

"Could be. The techs will test for that."

"I can see why you're so upset," Archie said, reaching out for his daughter's hand.

"Well, that's not the only reason," Betty replied sheepishly. "I've been ordered to stand down. The boss man doesn't want me looking into anything further given that I was involved with Andy and was friends with two of the three victims."

"Oh, poppycock," her father growled. "You aren't going to listen to him, are you?"

"Of course not," Betty replied, and then grinned.

Archie smiled back, his mood lifting.

"But it's on the Q-T, Dad. Got it," she said seriously.

"Got it," her father agreed.

"Seriously, Pops, no chatting about this with the boys over poker."

"I hear you, Angel puss," Archie muttered.

"And Dad…," she said.

"What?"

"You're a suspect as well," she finished.

Archie rolled his eyes at her.

Just then, a hooded figured sauntered out of Andy's laneway. The pockets of his jacket bulged. The figure glanced their way before striding forward, head down, scurrying away from them up North Shore Road.

Betty raced after the man, grabbed him by the shoulder and spun him around. Barnabas Whyte, billionaire condom factory owner and still operator, stared back at her with the same look he gave his first three wives when they caught him cheating.

"Barney, what on earth…," Archie gasped, catching up with Betty. His breathing was heavy, his eighty years finally starting to catch up with him.

"What are you doing skulking around in the bushes of an active crime scene," Betty demanded.

Barney pulled a mickey of moonshine from his pocket and took a swig before answering.

"Can't a man stop to take a piss on the way home," he countered.

Barney offered the mickey to Archie, and then to Betty. Both of them declined.

"A little early for the hard stuff," Archie admitted.

"It's never too early for my brew, Archie. You should try it in the morning with OJ. Anyway, I have a key. Andy's lawyer is or was my lawyer too. He asked me to look in on the house," Barney continued.

"Really," Betty added, eyebrows rising perceptibly.

"Yeah, really. You should be getting a call from him soon, Bets," the billionaire advised. He leered at her conspiratorially. "Now that we're talking about it, I forgot that I'm supposed to open up the house. I just got a call that a forensic team was on their way, or something to that effect. You know what that's all about?"

Betty's jaw set. Her blue eyes glittered, electricity crackling through them like Mary Shelley's Frankenstein. She glanced at her father and shook her head, not wanting him to breathe a word of what they had just been talking about. He nodded in understanding and made a closing a zipper motion in front of his mouth.

"So, you're acting Custodian of Andy's house then," she growled, not liking the idea of Barney routing around in Andy's house. Had she left anything there the last time she slept over? She couldn't remember.

"How come you never told me anything about this," Archie demanded. "For Pete's sake, I live just across the road, and you know Betty was involved with him."

"Didn't think it was important," Barney shrugged.

"Then why did you run," Archie asked angrily, folding his arms across his chest.

"I wasn't running. I just didn't want Betty to see me with my pecker hanging out."

"Too late for that," muttered Betty, glancing down at Barney's open fly.

"Blast," he grumbled, pulling up his zipper. His face brightened. "On the other hand, if you like what you see, Camille's gone for a few days."

"Criminy, Whyte, that's my daughter you're propositioning," Archie growled, his fists bunching.

"I'm a big girl, Dad," Betty soothed her father. "Keep your pecker in your pants, Barney."

Barney grinned.

"That's what Cam said just before I left the pub," Barney leered again.

Betty's cell phone rang. She glanced at the call display: Bentley, Smith and Conner Law. Who were they and what did they want?

"Hello," she said, answering the call.

"Who is it," her father mouthed to her.

She put a hand up to silence him.

"Say again," she said into the phone, her eyes widening in disbelief.

"Ah, that would be my lawyer right now," Barney said, elbowing Archie.

"What am I missing here," Archie whispered, totally confused.

"You'll see."

"Okay, thanks," Betty said into the phone. "Barney is with me right now. I'll get his key back after the transfer is complete." She paused, listening. "Yes, I have my own key."

Betty ended the call, a look of incredulity on her face.

"What was that all about," her father asked her.

"Andy changed his Will. He left the house and all its contents to me."

"Did he leave you any money," her father countered. Andy McDowell's wealth was rumored to rival that of Barney Whyte's.

"He donated everything else to charity," Betty replied with a shake of her head.

Archie's shoulders slumped, disappointed.

"Looks like you and your daughter are going to be neighbours," Barney beamed. "Ain't that a hoot?"

Betty scowled as her cell phone rang again. Was she ever going to get any time to herself today?

"Stew," she said, grumpily, "this better be good... Reggie and you found what? I can barely hear you... A body? Yes, drag it out of the surf, but don't do anything else. I'll be right there... What about Gertie? Look, you're breaking up. I'm on my way."

Betty hung up the cell.

"There's a body on the beach," Barney and Archie blurted out in unison.

"Uh-huh," Betty quipped. "This is turning out to be one heck of a day."

"What was that about Gertie," asked her father.

"Dunno. Stew's cell phone gave out. I'll give you a ring and let you know later."

Betty spun on her heels and started jogging back down

the road from which she just came. Whatever happened to that quiet sleepy little island she used to love, she wondered, increasing her pace.

***

Barney watched Betty go, admiring the lithe grace of the middle-aged woman whose short salt and pepper blond hair bobbed from side to side with each of her lengthy strides. Beatrice Bruce was a handsome woman, not pretty like his wife, but appealing in a deeply sensual way. He had wanted to take her to bed for a long time and had envied Andy McDowell.

"Keep your ugly thoughts to yourself, Barney. You proposition my daughter again and you'll answer to me," Archie growled. "It's not funny anymore."

Barney grinned. It never hurt to dream.

"It's all in jest, Arch, I assure you. I think the world of that girl of yours. I wish I had a daughter like that."

"Maybe if you hadn't cheated on all your wives within two months of marrying them, you'd have a family by now."

"Nah, I'm not father material and Cam's my last wife, I promise you that. I don't want kids, and neither does she. What can I say, it works for us. Sure you don't want a pull," Barney said, offering Archie a drink. "It'll help kill the pain of those busted up ribs of yours."

This time Archie took the mickey of moonshine from Barney's hand. He gulped down a stiff shot, gasping as it burned his throat. His cheeks flushed a deep crimson.

"Is that a hint of orange I taste, Barney?"

"Yep. That's why it goes great in OJ, or soda, or coffee, for that matter."

"Got any more?"

"As a matter of fact, I do," Barney chimed, pulling a second mickey of moonshine from his pocket. "This one's got a serious kick to it though."

Something's A Foot

Betty slowed her pace to a brisk walk when she reached the winding trail to the beach. An old Douglas fir towered over the trail, its skeletal top thumbing the sky. A black raven settled on one of the dead limbs. It looked down upon her. Its gaze was as intense as a Border collie watching her every move.

She shuddered, a chill sweeping through her spine as she realized that it must be the same one as from the cemetery. The movie, *The Crow*, sprang unbidden into her mind.

Betty turned her back on the bird and strode purposefully out onto the beach.

Stew and Reggie sat on a log, hunkered down against the bitterly cold northern wind that lifted her hair and made her button up her fleece jacket. There was an empty case of Molson Ale on the ground at the men's feet. Far from being drunk, the two men looked positively sober as they stared morosely at the body of the dead woman they had dragged up onto the rocks.

"Outside of pulling her out of the water, did you touch anything," Betty asked officiously.

"Thought we'd leave that to you," Stew commented dryly. "It's not exactly on my bucket list, fishing a body out of the water and all."

Reggie remained silent.

"What about you, Reg," she asked the quiet man.

"Nah, it's bad mojo," Reggie shivered. "I agree with the Navajo on that one. Don't want her spirit following me around. I got enough with Vi stoppin' by ta check on her Oscars."

Stew grinned sideways at the old fisherman, thinking his friend was joking.

Reggie took a sip of beer; his silence was his answer.

Stew stopped grinning.

Stew glanced sideways at Betty. Betty simply shrugged.

"How long has she been here," Betty continued, walking around the body, "or rather when did you first see her?"

Betty noticed that there were no cuts or abrasions on the woman's hands or wrists, but there was a purple bruise on the side of her face. Robbery wasn't a motive given the size of the diamond on her ring finger.

Crime of passion?

Accident?

"I guess it was about six beers ago," Reggie said, turning away from the tragic form that lay like a broken piece of driftwood on the rocky shore.

"We tried to lay her down all gentle like," Stew added, a gleam in his eye.

Betty noticed the way Stew was looking at the dead woman. There was no genuine grief or concern there. She knew instinctively that he was thinking about the money. People loved a good yarn, and this was going to be a dandy. It was his nature, rather like the story of the scorpion and the frog. Stew was the scorpion. In his eyes, what would the dead woman care if he made a little profit off her?

"And how long did the six beers take to drink, Reggie," Betty asked quietly, knowing that Reggie was Reggie just as much as Stew was Stew. If they were in the parable, Reggie would be the helpful frog offering to take the scorpion across the river. Reggie wasn't being smart with her, it was just his way. Despite his gruff and grizzled appearance, and his penchant for pot, Reggie was an honorable man.

"I'd guess about an hour, maybe more," he said, rubbing the stubble on his chin. "I came down here to think, ya know. All this dying on the island has plumb wore me out. And that raven over there, he's been dogging me for a couple of days."

Betty glanced at the golden eyed raven perched in the limbs of the eagle tree. The bird had been dogging her too, as Reggie so aptly put it.

"It's giving me the willies," Stew agreed, picking up a rock and taking aim.

"Don't do it, Stew, he's a harbinger," Reggie said, seizing the rock out of Stew's hand.

"A harbinger, you say," Stew replied.

"Aye, storm's a coming," Reggie muttered a warning.

The three of them stared at the raven. The raven stared back.

"Well, you boys did well," Betty interrupted the uneasy silence that had fallen over them.

She placed a comforting hand on Reggie's shoulder. She had never seen the man so down. He was usually such a good natured and happy sort, a peaceful man who she admired. That was why she never busted him and was happy to help him apply for a medical license to grow pot legally.

Reggie glanced upwards. He smiled thinly.

Betty knew he was grateful for her kind words.

"Oh, yeah, Bet, we almost forgot about Gertie," Stew chimed.

"What about Gert?"

"She found herself a sneaker," Stew continued.

"What's so special about this sneaker," Betty queried the two men, her focus on the well-dressed dead woman, or girl, as the case may be. She didn't look over twenty-four, if that.

And where was the woman's coat?

It was cold out here.

And where was her lifejacket?

Folks didn't wear lifejackets on the cruise ships, but this wasn't cruise ship season. The only boats in the Strait og Georgia at this time of year were fishing boats and private yachts. This woman definitely didn't fall off of a fishing boat.

"There was a foot in it," Stew said, smacking his lips in satisfaction.

"Aye, sawed off at the ankle is what it looked like," Reggie added for good measure. "Course, I only saw it for a few seconds as Gertie ran by with it."

"Oh, Lord, not another one," Betty said, her shoulders

drooping forward. If Gertrude had found another severed foot in a sneaker, that would make it the ninth one to be discovered on the coast.

A ship's horn blared loudly as the weekly barge rounded the point, heading towards the dock at Herald Bay. There were two police cruisers, two unmarked SUV's, three forensic vans, and a large moving van on board. The woman picked the perfect time to wash up on Seal Island.

Timing was everything, Betty thought dryly.

"Can you two stay with the body for a few minutes," Betty asked them.

"Sure," Stew agreed, "but let Gwen know, will you, Bet? I don't want a tongue lashing just because Reggie and me are performing our civic duty."

"I will," Betty agreed, bracing herself for the show that was about to begin.

Betty tugged her cell phone from her pocket and called her detachment. It was best to go through proper channels rather than calling Doc Forester directly. She already knew he was in one of the vehicles on the barge. He had told her as much. She would let the Watch Commander notify the forensics crew about the body on the beach Gertrude's precious find.

"No," she said into the phone after what was proving to be a frustrating and an unnecessarily lengthy conversation, "I don't have the foot, just witnesses. I have to go find my pig first." And then, "Yes, the body is secure. Forensics is just arriving on the island on another matter. I'll go and fetch them. Just have the Watch Commander call Doc Forester right away."

Betty hung up, a dark scowl on her face. She dialed her father next.

"Dad, I need your help down at the landing. Gertrude's got herself a prize. Fast as you can, Pops."

Betty hung up, and then raced over the rocks, heading towards the ferry landing. She squared her shoulders and braced herself to be ready for anything... she hoped.

***

Betty stood outside the Bristling Boar Pub, hands on her hips, furious at the pot-bellied pig, and even more furious at the turn of events that landed her in this predicament. The line of police and forensic vehicles pulled off the barge and formed a large semi-circle in the pub parking lot.

A moving van slowly drove past, its gears grinding, and greasy smoke billowing out the tailpipe. A sign on the side of it said, 'McDonald's Poultry Farm'. A taciturn man in a cowboy hat drove it. His face although pleasant, seemed as grim as the afternoon it was turning out to be.

A youthful woman with long dreadlocked auburn hair stared with timid eyes out the passenger window. She tentatively lifted a hand to wave at Betty as the van rumbled by, but a word from the man stopped her in mid-wave.

It was a small island. The couple was expected. Frank and Rainbow McDonald, the new owners of Summer River's homestead, weren't happy to share the barge with a crowd of police officers, detectives, and forensic technicians.

Betty returned her attention to the crowd of pub patrons chasing Gertrude around and around the grassy landing in front of the pub, valiantly trying to retrieve the red sneaker from the pig's mouth. The cow stood idly by watching the Keystone Cops scene unfold.

The McDonald's van pulled over to the side of the road. A window opened and a Blue heeler's head popped out of the window, the dog's eyes bright with interest. The McDonalds leaned forward to catch the excitement from the safety of the cab.

Morris Tweedsmuir, easily the most agile of all the men, dodged right and then left, trying to feint the pig out. He was as unsuccessful as Ernie Bates, a Paul Bunyon of a man, who though strong as an ox, was not so swift. Had Ernie been able to catch Gertrude, he would have lifted the pig off its feet in one fell swoop. A group of fishermen who had ambled up from the docks joined in the fun. A multitude of flapping gumboots and wind-milling arms was the result.

"Gertrude, stop this immediately," Betty ordered. "Give it here."

The pig ignored her, running this way and that, defiant, coat bristling, the red sneaker with the severed foot in it dripping with pig spit. Gertrude spun right, and then left, avoiding the outstretched hands of her pursuers. Curses rumbled through the air like thunder claps, each one growing louder and more profane.

Corporal Peter Singh, a friend of Betty's, stepped out of the driver's side of one cruiser. Doc Forester, the coroner, stepped out of the passenger side, his shoulders bent with age. He had carried the weight of the job on his shoulders for more years than he could count.

For a large beast, the pot-bellied pig was remarkably agile. Gertrude plowed down man after man, refusing to give up the goods.

Forester burst out laughing.

"It's not funny, Doc, we need that foot," Singh grumbled.

"I know, Pete," Forester chuckled. "She is just so darned amusing. I think I might adopt one when I retire."

"You'll never retire, Doc," Betty said, her face softening as she approached the pair. She had stayed with Forester for several months after finding the courage to file for divorce. He was the only one, outside of her father, who knew about her ex-husband's abuse.

"Dad should be down shortly. Gertie will listen to him," Betty added.

"Seems you've got your hands full again, Bet," Singh said. "I hear you've got a floater too."

"Yeah, I'm beginning to think this island's cursed," she replied, sweeping an errant lock of cinnamon blond hair from her face.

Inspector Tom Powder stepped out of the second cruiser, his salt and pepper black hair, broad face and open expression, a stark contrast to his partner's. Corporal Ben Hammerton's wiry Nordic frame was all muscle and carefully checked aggression.

"Sergeant Bruce, I presume," Tom Powder said, extending a hand.

"Just call me Betty," she said, shaking the offered hand.

"That your pig," Hammerton sneered.

"My father's," Betty answered, taking an instant dislike to the arrogant inexperienced detective.

"I understand that you're on the Task Force dealing with these dismembered feet," Powder commented, motioning towards the running pig, the laugh lines around his eyes crinkling with contained mirth.

"Unfortunately," Betty agreed.

Powder chuckled as a bull dog of a fisherman grabbed the pig around the waist. Another man then grabbed him around the waist causing the pig to spin around in circles, dragging the two men behind it, the men's feet flying in alternating directions.

"Guess we'll let you deal with that," he guffawed.

Betty nodded in agreement, taking the detective's measure, and liking what she saw. "Ahhh, here comes my father now."

Archie drove his rusted old Dodge pickup truck into the yard, swerving to avoid the McDonald's large one ton van. He parked in front of the pub. Archie and the Dodge looked like they had been through a tornado's soak and rinse cycle.

Betty groaned inwardly. Her father was clearly loaded. Damn Barney and his moonshine, she grimaced, gritting her teeth.

"Gertrude, you come 'ere right now," the old man bellowed, his speech slurred.

The pig darted between Tweedsmuir and Bates. The two men collided and dropped to the ground. Three police officers jumped into the fray as the errant pig jogged past them heading for Archie. She bulldozed one officer over, leaving him sitting dazed on the ground. The other two leapt out of the way, deciding pig wrangling wasn't in their job description.

"You want to take the lead on the body on the beach, Betty," Singh asked woodenly.

"Yeah, Sergeant in Charge says it's my case. I'll take Doc and two techs down to recover the body once we get this dealt with," Betty agreed.

"That might take some time," Powder observed.

The pig did an abrupt reversal, skipping away from Archie's outstretched arms. She jogged a few laps round the placid Jersey cow.

"Good grief, I've had enough of this," Hammerton hissed.

The young detective strode past them, pulled a stun gun from beneath his jacket, and took aim at the pig.

"You jerk," Betty screamed. "Don't you dare taser my pig."

Betty lashed at the taser in Hammerton's hand, but was too late. The twin taser ends arched through the air. The shot went wild. The two stunners missed the pig and hit the Jersey cow. Peaches bawled and dropped like a rock. She lay on the ground, twitching.

"You've killed Peaches," Ernie Bates roared.

The crowd froze. Shocked faces turned towards the motionless cow lying on the ground, legs straight out like a child's plastic play toy, the twitches ending when the taser's electric jolts ceased.

The pig dropped the sneaker from its mouth and squealed in dismay. Gertrude rushed to her friend's side. The cow didn't move, despite the pig's none too gentle urging.

Tweedsmuir snatched the sneaker out of the mud and tossed it like a hot potato to one of the cops standing by. The cop caught it in mid-air. He raced over to his cruiser, placed the sneaker and amputated foot in an evidence bag, and threw it onto the back seat, slamming the door shut behind him, his lips moving as he silently prayed the pig wouldn't notice it was missing.

Gertrude switched her attention from the downed cow to the young wiry police detective. Intelligent beady eyes zeroed in on him.

"Run," Betty yelled.

Gertrude charged.

"What the...," Hammerton croaked, startled, drawing his side arm from its holster.

Gertie, stop," Betty yelled, placing herself between Hammerton and the raging pig.

Fishermen and farmers danced out of the way like ballerinas in gumboots performing Swan Lake. Nobody wanted to get trampled by the irate pig.

Gertrude tried to zigzag around Betty, her rage fixed on the broad shouldered blond man who had tasered her best friend.

Tom Powder snatched the pistol from his partner's hand.

"Have you lost your mind, kid," he shouted at the young inspector.

"It's a bloody cow," Hammerton hollered back.

"For God sakes run," Betty shouted.

Hammerton stood his ground, as stubborn as the pot-bellied pig bearing down on him.

Betty moved right and then left, quickly matching the pig's feints, blocking Gertrude's progress.

"Dad, help me out here," she yelled at her father.

Archie sprang into action, the moonshine haze that had befuddled his thoughts dissipating. He grabbed the pig's harness from the back of the truck and ran to his daughter's aid. He threw himself on top of the pig, quickly fastening the harness around Gertrude's ample belly as Betty wrangled the pig's head into her body.

"I'll check on the cow," Forester called over the hubbub, pulling a black leather bag from the back of one of the forensic vans. He moved swiftly to the fallen cow, medical bag in hand.

Morris Tweedsmuir spat into the dirt, his face seething with anger. The rest of the men gathered around the fallen cow wore severe expressions. If Peaches died, and right now it appeared she had, someone was going to pay and that someone was a haughty young cop with an itchy trigger finger.

"Oye, Gertie, behave yourself," Archie admonished the pig.

Archie and Betty hauled the angry pig over to the old Dodge, tied a rope to the harness ring, and then fastened the rope to the rear bumper. They prayed the rope would hold.

Forester knelt in the dirt beside the cow. His knees popped with arthritis. With a groan he bent over and placed a hand on the cow's chest. He pulled a stethoscope out of his bag and listened to where he thought the cow's heart would be. Forty years on the job and this was a first.

"She's alive, just stunned," the coroner advised the group of men circling him.

The group let out a collective sigh of relief. As one, they turned to face the RCMP detective who had stunned Peaches, anger replacing the concern for the downed cow.

"I suggest you get back in that cruiser quick as Peter Pan," Powder commented dryly.

"And lock the doors," Singh advised.

"It's a frigging cow," Hammerton sulked.

"And that's a lynch mob," Tom warned him.

Inspector Hammerton climbed into the passenger side of one cruiser, his face gloomy but unrepentant.

"You men fall back," Powder motioned to the officers looking to him for guidance. Not a man there wanted to deal with the furious group of farmers and fishermen whose simmering distrust of the police Hammerton had fueled into a tide of glowering resentment.

"Come on now, up you get," Doc Forester said to the cow as the coroner stood shakily to his feet.

Peaches sat up, bawled, and then licked her lips.

"Up you go, Peaches," Morris Tweedsmuir encouraged the cow, all misdeeds of the past forgotten.

The cow climbed slowly to its feet.

Gertrude yanked hard on her harness. The bumper groaned. The truck rocked back and forth. The pig increased the pressure until finally the harness's buckles snapped in two. She squealed with joy, free at last, and ran to her friend's side.

Betty moaned in frustration.

Her father looked at her and shrugged helplessly.

At the far side of the landing, the McDonald's van roared into life. The dog barked. Rainbow tugged it back inside. She wiped a tear from her eye and flashed a peace sign at Betty.

"The fun's over everyone," Betty said to the men. "Thanks for your help. Tell Gwen the pints are on me, but just one mind you."

"Hurrah," the men all cheered.

The group turned and headed for the pub, slapping each other on the back for a job well done. Morris and Ernie glowered at the police.

"You too, gentlemne."

"Sure we should be leaving you with this lot," Morris offered, waving a hand towards the police officers and forensic crew.

"I'll be fine and my dad can look after Gert and Peaches. I do believe the walk home will do him good, won't it, Pops?"

"Expect it will, Angel," Archie replied sheepishly. He winked at his daughter.

Morris and Ernie strode off towards the pub.

"Oye, Morris," Betty called to the bearded farmer, "let Gwen know that I've enlisted Stew's help down at the beach, will you? I'll send him up shortly."

"Will do, Bet," Morris replied as he and Ernie leapt up the stairs to the pub two at a time.

"Thanks for checking on Peaches, Doc," Archie said after a moment, glancing longingly after Morris and Ernie.

"No problem, Archie," Forester replied, packing up his bag.

"You keep that young 'un under control," Archie advised Tom Powder, "or we'll make him walk the plank."

"I will, sir, although I have to admit the thought of him walking the plank sort of appeals to me," Powder replied.

"Ready to go see that body now that the fun's over, Doc," Betty asked the coroner.

"Lead the way, my dear," he said.

"I suggest you take that hot-headed partner of yours up to Andy's place and tell him to stay there," Betty advised Tom. "We don't need any more bodies than what we've got right now."

Tom grinned.

"I will."

"After you've dropped him off, you're welcome to mosey on

back here and join us on the beach. An extra set of eyes won't hurt. We've got a good mile of beach to comb for evidence," Betty offered.

"I just might do that," Powder replied before stalking off to join his partner.

Doc Forester, two police officers, and three forensic technicians, joined Betty on her trek back down to the beach where the woman's body was being guarded from scavenger birds by a pot growing fisherman and a lascivious pub owner.

The day was just getting better and better, Betty shuddered.

Perched in the eagle tree towering over the beach trail, the raven watched with interest.

The Clueless and the Sublime

"Off you go, Stew," Betty said to the pub owner as she approached the two men. "Gwen's got a full house up there."

"I don't mind staying to help," Stew offered amiably.

"That's okay, I've got back-up now. I'll get a proper statement from you later," she replied, watching the man's eyes glitter like a kid on Christmas morning as he took in the forensic team, the slump-shouldered coroner, and the two dour faced cops following along behind her. She knew exactly what the man was thinking: beer, money, a good yarn to tell, and a little bump and tickle later.

What women saw in the aging round-faced barrel-chested pub owner was beyond Betty. The thought of the gorgeous writer and real estate agent, Tiffany Hyde-White, sharing a bed with him was abhorrent. Why Gwen stayed with him was even more of a puzzle?

"You officers cordon off this area from the trailhead down to the high tide line," Forester ordered. "Jason, you're with me. Snap as many photos as you can. Charlie and Jeremy, start working the beach. See what you can find. Put the hustle in hustle. Looks like a storm is coming in and any potential evidence that there might be will get washed away within the next hour, I expect."

The two techs nodded and immediately began sifting through the seaweed and debris close to the body while the third tech started snapping photos.

"Ya got a good sniffer there, Doc," Reggie said, watching the storm clouds gathering to the north-east, "but I think you got less time than that."

"How long you figure," Betty asked the bleary-eyed fisherman.

"Maybe a half hour," he croaked.

Reggie's callused hands shook perceptibly as he tugged his toque down lower over his forehead. The last time Betty had seen Reggie this devastated was at Eliza Bone's funeral.

"If Reggie says we got half an hour, we got half an hour," Doc Forester called to his techs.

"Why don't you head up to the pub with Stew and have a pint on me," Betty said gently to the older fisherman.

"Aye, come on, Reg, I'll draw you a pint of the good stuff," Stew offered.

"Ya sure, Bet," asked Reggie. "I kind'a figured maybe I should stay since she washed up at my feet and all. Someone needs ta look out fer her, ya know what I mean?"

"That's kind of you, Reggie, but I promise you that Doc Forester and I will do right by her," Betty comforted the man.

"We will that," Doc Forester agreed.

Reggie sighed wearily and turned towards the cordoned off path. The officers had already strung yellow and black police tape across the trail. The two officers stood sentinel on either side of the path way.

"Let them pass," Betty told the officers. "I'll swing by later for a statement from the two of you."

"Come on, mate," Stew urged his friend.

Reggie turned his piercing grey eyes skyward. The raven was gone from the top of the eagle tree. The wind stirred his grey locks. He shivered.

The two officers lifted the tape for the two men.

Reggie nodded a goodbye to Betty and Doc Forester before heading off to the pub, Stew Mann striding jauntily along beside him.

"Funny fellow that," Forester commented wryly.

"Which one," Betty asked softly.

"Both," Forester answered, offering Betty a pair of latex gloves. "Anyway, time is of the essence. What are your thoughts on this, Sergeant?"

"Well," Betty said, squatting down beside the body, "it wasn't a robbery. That rock on her finger must be worth a fortune. She isn't wearing a coat or lifejacket, so she must have either been killed somewhere else and tossed in the strait or she fell off a boat. Look at her nails. That is a custom job if I ever saw one."

"Are those little unicorns painted on her fingernails?"

"Rainbows and unicorns. Didn't end up a rainbow-colored day for her," Betty said, lifting one of the dead woman's hands to examine her fingertips. "Doesn't look like she struggled with her attacker. None of her nails are broken."

"Given her attire, she must have been on a yacht," the Coroner agreed.

"That's what I was thinking too. Definitely well-to-do. I checked with dispatch and there are no missing women matching her age and description listed right now, but maybe she hasn't been reported missing yet," Betty added.

Doc Forester gently rolled the body over.

"No ID of any sort," he said, checking her pockets. "She hasn't been in the water long. Not much bloating."

"Yeah, that's what I figured," Betty agreed. "I'm guessing she's mid-twenties, maybe late twenties."

"If her body was dumped, it would have had to have been on this island somewhere or maybe the big island as I honestly don't think she's been in the water for more than eight hours, if that. Once Jason has completed some tests and we have body and water temperature, we can get her back to the lab. I'll get you a full report as soon as possible. Given the length of beach we have to cover and the incoming storm, I'm not convinced we'll find anything of much help as far as evidence. That's the problem with floaters, especially in salt water; the evidence gets washed away or corrupted pretty quickly."

"And in the meantime," Betty continued, glancing at the two techs combing the beach, "I have a severed foot covered with pig DNA to deal with."

"And I have a crime scene investigation at your beau's house to oversee," Forster completed.

"Apparently it's my house now."

"Say what?"

"Andy willed his house to me," Betty sighed, standing up. "I got a call from his lawyer about a half an hour ago."

"That does put a new spin on things. You're going to have to be careful, my dear," the old man eyed her. "I know you. Don't interfere in Powder's investigation. He's a good man. That Hammerton is a jerk, but Powder is very capable. You have enough on your plate right now and getting suspended won't help you at all."

"I hear you," Betty said, her face grim.

"But will you listen?"

"Probably not," she conceded.

***

"Kid, working with you is like being on the worldwide web. It's making me whiter, wider, and wiser, every day," Tom Powder chided his partner. "Pretty soon my wife will trade me in for a younger model and my kids won't know me."

"I still don't get what the big deal was. The cow is fine. The pig gave up the foot. It was a win-win."

"Yeah, win-win, just like the group of fishermen who wanted to make you walk the plank and the farmers that wanted to lynch you."

Tom leaned against the black granite countertop, latex gloves on his hands, and coverall booties over his shoes. The techs were everywhere, white suits as bright as the subway tiled back splash and painfully white walls. It was the coldest, most uninviting kitchen he had ever been in.

It told him loads about Andrew McDowell, the dead man they were investigating. Perfectionist, totalitarian, self-absorbed, and obsessive, was just a few of the man's characteristics that sprang to mind.

Powder's interest was piqued when he was handed the case. Every officer on the mainland had heard about Sergeant Betty

Bruce's investigations into a series of bizarre deaths on Seal Island and her infamous pot-bellied pig and its Jersey cow cohort. What he couldn't figure out was how she got involved with Andy McDowell. After meeting her in person, he found it even harder to believe that this seemingly intelligent woman would fall for some young stud. She didn't strike him as the lonely heart type either. The gumboots, lumberjack jacket, jeans, and glint of silver in her hair, made it clear that appearance wasn't important to her, and neither was money.

Thanks to his wife, he knew all about McDowell. McDowell's torrid romances littered the house. She was his number one fan, going gaga at just the mere mention of his name, her eyes glittering, and her face flushing like she'd just bit into a hot tamale. It reminded him of that Stephen King book, *Misery*. Mrs Powder was devastated when news of the author's death hit the media. He wondered if she'd wail that much at his funeral?

Was that it?

Was Sergeant Betty Bruce McDowell's number one fan too?

"I hear this dude was some hotshot romance writer," Hammerton muttered, idly opening a cupboard and rifling through the boxes of corn flakes and granola.

"Do you mind," a tech said angrily.

"Let us do our job, will you," another whined.

Powder sighed.

"Come on, let's check upstairs and let these guys work," Tom said, walking off towards the living room.

The techs rolled their eyes at each other and then went back to work taking food and water samples.

Powder entered the living room and stopped short. The room was as sterile as the kitchen: pristine white walls, glass topped black enamel tables, an uncomfortable looking couch, and black and white photos of skyscrapers and cathedrals on the wall. There wasn't one family photo anywhere, not on a table, a cabinet top or a wall. The décor didn't match the old-world charm of the grand old house, and it didn't jibe with an author of torchy sex riddled historical romances.

"Doesn't add up," Tom mumbled under his breath.

"What," his partner asked, brushing past him and heading for the stairs.

"I was just thinking that this place doesn't look like any drug house I've ever seen," Powder said, rubbing a hand through his short-cropped hair.

"You thought the LSD would be laid out on a table all nice and neat for us or maybe piled high in a candy jar? Come on, partner," Ben scoffed. "This guy was smart. Probably has it squirreled away in a wall or floor safe somewhere in the house."

"All I'm saying is that this house is too neat for someone with as much dope in their system as this guy had."

"Maybe Sergeant Bruce cleaned the place up before we came. I hear they were all hot and heavy. You know, December-Spring romance, or whatever they call it," Hammerton smirked.

"Lay off, Ben, Bruce's got some serious commendations to her credit," cautioned the older detective. "She's a cop's cop if ever there was one."

"Doesn't mean she didn't like getting her pipes cleaned by this dude and then came over and literally cleaned the pipes," the young man stated coldly.

"Criminy, Hammerton, you're a jerk sometimes."

Tom Powder frowned. The kid was right. Whether or not he wanted to believe it, Sergeant Bruce may have cleaned up after her boyfriend. Still, she didn't strike him as the type to hide or alter evidence, especially when it came to drugs.

The two men climbed the stairs to the second floor.

The other thing that bothered him, he realized as he stopped at the top of the landing, was the LSD. LSD wasn't the drug of choice these days; although, it was making a comeback. Crack, yes. Cocaine, definitely, and Fentanyl was an epidemic, but LSD, not so much.

The LSD that was in McDowell's system was lethal, top quality with a mix not seen since the seventies, Doc Forester had told him.

McDowell was so high on LSD and his brain so distorted

from the lead poisoning, that he was definitely out of his mind enough to kill three people, but hardly in good enough shape to rig the deaths to look like accidents, plus continue writing his next best selling bodice ripper romance novel. Both he and Doc Forester agreed that it was a conundrum.

Were those three deaths truly bizarre accidents? Was McDowell so deluded that he really believed he killed all three women? What about the Sergeant? Was she right and the deaths were the work of a serial killer? And if so, was the serial killer still at large?

There were a lot of questions that needed answering.

"I found the safe," his partner called from a side room.

Powder followed his voice to the office.

Finally, a room he could relate to.

Rectangular marks and discoloration on the ceiling in the office-library showed that two rooms had been turned into one giant one. Floor to ceiling oak bookcases lined two walls. There were books on everything from gardening to medieval history, raising chickens to war machines, Tolstoy to Ludlum, Tom Clancy to Stephen King. Dark brown hardwood floors bore fifty years of scuff marks. A frayed Indian rug covered up the worst ones. An antique writer's desk sat beneath a stained-glass window, the view of the pasture below and the mountain to the north was breathtaking. A tattered over-stuffed recliner chair rested in front of a rock mantled fireplace.

Hammerton sat at the desk, an open drawer by his side. Rubber gloves encased his hands.

"Found it. It's got a combination lock," he said, examining the hidden safe inside the drawer. He tugged on the safe's handle. "That's weird. It's not locked."

The detective pulled open the small safe's door and then pulled out the contents.

Powder wandered over and examined the sheaves of paper and yellowed letters. He assumed the letters were McDowell's mother's keepsakes. Her name was on a wrinkled copy of an old Will. There was also a small carved jewelry box made of cedar, plus what looked like a draft of a new book.

Powder opened the jewelry box. There was a dozen pair of gold and silver cufflinks, a lady's gold wedding band, and nothing else.

"What do you think this manuscript's worth," Hammerton asked.

"More than yours and my salary combined," Tom responded.

"No drugs though," the junior detective said. "Maybe there's another safe?"

"Maybe there isn't, and he wasn't a junkie at all. Maybe someone ruffied him," Powder mused aloud.

"Or maybe he liked to take a trip when he was writing, and he ran out."

Hammerton flipped through the pages of the manuscript.

"This is strange."

"What is," Powder asked, his attention drawn to the window where a hawk flew lazy circles in the sky.

"There is more than one set of handwriting in the margins in this manuscript," Ben noted. "Think we should bag it and tag it?"

"Probably those are just editor's notes. Note it in our logbook, but put it back in the safe. It's up to the estate's attorney to decide what to do with it. This guy was too famous to go leafing through his unpublished work like you're doing now."

Hammerton ignored him.

"Strange that the safe would be open like this," Hammerton noted.

"We'll get the techs to dust it. Doc Forester should be along shortly. We'll see what he has to say."

"You going to go down to the beach and check out that floater," the callow man asked.

"No, there is enough of a mystery here to sort through and Sergeant Bruce is more than capable of handling it," Powder said, retrieving the manuscript he had just told his partner to leave alone. Hammerton was right. There was more than one person's handwriting present on the pages; in fact, it looked like three distinct people had made notes and changes to it: McDowell, his editor, and an unidentified third person?

"You mind your manners when she gets here," Powder advised, placing the manuscript back in the drawer.

His partner grinned up at him.

That wasn't a good sign.

Tom sighed wearily.

Old McDonald Had A Farm

"Well, here we are," Frank McDonald said, breaking into a grin that lit his brooding face up like the fourth of July.

"Did you see that cop taser that poor cow," Rainbow sobbed. "How could anyone be so mean?"

"Yeah, honey, I sure did. I bet the folks that own her will need your help."

"I can't imagine what it has done to her psyche. It makes me shiver just thinking about it," the soft-spoken woman cried out.

"Definitely not a grand way to start off our first day on the island, but we'll make the best of it," Frank consoled his wife.

The two of them stepped out of the big panel van, their black and white spotted heeler jumping out right after them. The dog took off barking, tail wagging, and nose to the ground. The couple looked at their new home.

"Blue, don't go too far," Frank called after the dog.

The dog raced back, circling around the young couple, barking with glee.

"I can't believe nobody rescued those dried herbs I see hanging in the barn's doorway," Rainbow said, pointing towards the open barn door where bunches of dried herbs, brittle with age and black with mould, swayed gently in the breeze.

"I expect they just missed them," Frank answered. "Look, the fields are mulched. That was nice."

Inside the large fenced acreage, the black earth was covered in hay and leaf mulch to protect the soil. Several rows of lavender, thyme, rosemary, lemon balm, and mint were still green and healthy thanks to the mild winter.

Rainbow smiled.

"Look at those herbs! No one removed them. Good golly gosh," she said, fairly vibrating with happiness.

"The Realtor said he hired a local fisherman, some fella named Reggie Phoenix, to look after the property. Looks like he did a good job of keeping the fences up and the deer out," Frank said approvingly.

"I can't wait to move our stuff in, but I want to pick some sage and perform a smudging ceremony first," Rainbow crooned, throwing her arms around her husband's neck.

"I think that is a righteous idea, babe, given the Realtor said that poor lady died somewhere here on the property," Frank said, snuggling up to his wife.

Frank swung his wife around in a circle causing her skirts to billow out around her like a colorful sail. They both laughed.

"Ole Blue's gonna love it here, aren't you fella," Frank added, plopping his wife back down on the ground. He reached down and rubbed the dog's ears. The dog grinned up at him.

Behind them, between the fenced off fields, the barn, and the house, a circular patch of bare earth marked where the stone angel had once stood. The rock walled fountain that had stood in front of it was still there. Brackish water trickled over its sides creating a muddy mess around the fountain's base.

"Happy new home day, honey," Frank cried, scooping Rainbow up in his arms and carrying her across the front porch of the log house.

Rainbow opened the front door, and her husband carried her into the house like the recent bride that she was.

"Oh, oh," her husband muttered as they crossed the threshold. He set Rainbow on her feet.

The Realtor had assured them that the house would be emptied out.

The kitchen was as Summer had left it. There was a hand pottered teal green tea pot set to one side of the stove, two china teacups beside it. Tins of Summer's herbal teas stretched all along one counter. The honey pot was open and sticky with the carcasses of dead flies. A loaf of green moldy bread also lay on the kitchen counter.

Pictures of Summer River hung on the walls: Summer in the garden, selling herbs at the local farmer's market, and kneeling in front of a giant stone angel a grey tabby cat at her feet, a shy smile on her face. Beside that was a picture of the young girl in a sarong, flanked by two old men. Rainbow shuddered. The leer on one of the old men's faces was pure evil.

"I guess that caretaker dude only looked after the farm itself," Frank grumbled. "This is the same as when we viewed it."

The dog barged into the house.

"Oh, no you don't, Blue," Frank admonished the dog. "Out you go."

The dog whimpered as Frank ushered him back outside.

Rainbow ignored them both and wandered through the kitchen and into the compact living room.

A handmade quilt with a seaside theme lay neatly folded on the futon couch and shells of every size and type decorated the window ledges. A pile of firewood was stacked in a u-shaped iron ring beside the woodstove.

The one and only bedroom was on the far side of the living room.

Frank walked past Rainbow and into the bedroom.

The sheets were tucked in so tight on the double bed you could bounce a quarter off them. Summer's clothes hung neatly on hangers in the closet.

"Looks like we got our work cut out for us," Frank complained.

"I'll feel more comfortable once we wish Miss River a safe passage to the other side and thank her for allowing us into her home."

"Ditto. We'll pack her stuff up as we un-pack," Frank said, forcefully. "I'll call the Realtor in the morning and tell him to come pick her stuff up when we're done. I'll go see if there is a dry space to store it in the barn. I don't want to put it in our truck."

Frank kissed his wife on the cheek.

Rainbow heard him open and close the door in the kitchen as he left the house.

Rainbow wrapped her arms around her body and hugged herself. This was so sad. The family hadn't cared enough about this lady to pack up her things.

Didn't she have any friends?

Rainbow and Frank had fallen in love with the small log home and the amazing oceanfront acreage the minute they laid eyes upon it. The energy of the property was amazing. Rainbow knew that this was the place for them. There was no place like it on the mainland, at least nothing that they could afford.

Frank's family had helped with the down payment. Rainbow had grown up in the foster care system with no family worth knowing. Instead of letting her experiences make her bitter, she turned inward, and went on a journey of self discovery. Her travels took her to India and then Nepal, Bali, and China where she studied and practiced buddhism. She found peace in Mother Nature and discovered her true calling. She embraced it and started her own pet psychic business when she returned to the west coast.

That was how she met Frank. His heeler stopped eating. Numerous trips to the vet proved fruitless, the dog had continued to refuse food and was extremely lethargic. Frank had heard about Rainbow from a friend and brought Blue in to see her. Blue told her right away what the problem was. The old dog that he had bonded with at the doggy daycare had died. Frank was too busy for him and he was tired of being alone all the time. Once Frank started taking Blue to work with him, the heeler bounced back, started eating again and enjoying life.

Frank and Rainbow married six months later.

Rainbow couldn't wait to start an organic farm and poultry business with her husband. Frank believed that the real money was in raising specialty birds like quail, partridge and duck. The farm was a dream come true, at least, it was supposed to be.

Rainbow returned to the kitchen and looked at the pictures on the wall. She fingered the one of Summer sitting in front of the stone angel. It was obvious that the empty space in front of the house beside the fountain was where the angel had sat. At least the family had wanted something of the dead woman's.

The hairs on the back of her neck stood up.

Someone was watching her.

Rainbow spun on her heels. A doe-eyed girl in flowing skirts, gumboots, and a sequined Gypsy scarf, greeted her with a gentle wave of a ghostly hand.

The wispy figure pointed towards the bedroom, beckoning Rainbow to follow her.

Rainbow had no fear of the woman's ghost; in fact, Rainbow felt blessed that Summer River felt comfortable enough to show herself to her. She would never turn away a person, an animal, or a ghost in need. Rainbow breathed a sigh of relief, thankful that there were no ill feelings emanating from the spectral form that glided through the living room and into the bedroom.

The ghost kneeled and pointed under the bed.

Rainbow strode purposefully into the bedroom and lifted the bed skirts where several homemade cardboard boxes were tucked away in the dark amidst the dust bunnies and fur balls. Rainbow pulled one box out and turned to the ghost.

"Is this the one," she asked the apparition, but the ghost was gone.

Rainbow stood up and then sat on the bed. She opened the box.

Dozens of photos filled the box: Summer at various ages, a happy couple wearing hip hugger jeans and tie dyed shirts, and a boy that looked just like her, but he had a cruel set to his mouth and a deep scowl on his face. Rainbow assumed that he must be related, a brother maybe. The glowing hippy couple must be Summer's parents.

Rainbow ran a finger over a more recent photo of a strikingly handsome man with sweat soaked curly hair and a muscled physique. He held a hammer in one hand and grinned mischievously into the camera. He looked like one of those models one sees on the covers of those lusty romance books stacked beside the till at the supermarket.

The best picture though, in Rainbow's eyes, was a candid

photo of Summer, her arms wrapped around the neck of a freckle faced fellow who stared adoringly into her loving eyes. The photo was smudged and covered in fingerprints. Rainbow wondered what had happened to that man and why he hadn't come to pick up the dead woman's things.

Perhaps the smudges were tears?

Maybe he was gone too?

Rainbow found a small diary beneath the photos. The pages were dog-eared. The giant sunflower painted on the cover was faded with age.

Fascinated, Rainbow forgot about her trip to the garden to pick sage and sat down on the bed. She tucked her legs beneath her, leaned against the pillows, wrapped the comforter around her slim body, and opened the diary.

***

Frank pulled down the rotting herbs that hung from the barn's rafters and tossed them into a corner. Blue rummaged through them but found nothing of interest.

"What do you think of your new home, Blue," he asked the dog.

The dog whined and wagged his tail. His nostrils quivered and his eyes brightened. He bolted out of the barn, barking.

Frank laughed, thrilled that his dog was so happy.

He had big plans for this property and was eager to get started. The previous owner's things still being in the house was a setback, but a minor one, all things considered.

He looked around the big open space, his face breaking into a schoolboy grin.

A nearly new John Deere tractor sat under a tarp at the end of the barn. Beside it was chain harrows for harrowing the fields, a small snowplow blade, and a posthole digging attachment. There were a couple of chainsaws, several rolls of chicken wire, fencing materials, and all the tools he would need to enlarge the chicken coup and build more outbuildings for his birds. Frank figured that since no one had removed them, the rule of finders-keepers applied.

The rest of the barn was unused. It would be easy to build a proper rendering area for the fowl in the back of the barn. He already had the permits pre-filled out. He just had to build it and get the Health Inspection done.

Frank turned his attention to the large storage room beside the main entrance. He opened the heavy door and walked inside.

"Wowsers, Rainbow is gonna flip," he gasped.

Huge glass mason jars filled with dried flowers and herbs of every kind lined three walls of the room. Neatly printed on the jars in black felt marker were names like hibiscus, comfrey, marigold, mint, lemon balm, chamomile, and many others. His wife would be ecstatic.

A hot press for sealing the herbs inside the marketing packages, boxes for shipping, a postage machine, and measuring cups and spoons of all sizes were neatly arranged on a bench along the far wall. There were boxes of unused labels and packages with *River's Herbal Home Remedy* stamped on them.

He opened a couple of the larger shipping boxes and discovered more of the same. He idly wondered why the business hadn't sold. From what the Realtor told them; it was a real money maker. Maybe Rainbow could start the company back up under a new name? She had done okay with her pet psychic business on the mainland, but she wasn't sure how it was going to do on such a small island. This would be a great project for her, he realized.

He spotted a battered plastic milk crate buried beneath a couple of boxes. He yanked the crate out from under the boxes. There was a series of smaller mason jars stacked one on top of the other inside the crate. He lifted one jar up and looked at the clear liquid inside.

What on earth was it, he wondered?

He wrestled the top of one of the mason jars off and took a sniff. The stringent smell of alcohol that greeted him burned his nostrils and made him stagger backwards.

Frank grinned and wiped his nose on his coat sleeve. He knew that smell. His uncle made moonshine every Christmas. It wasn't as strong as this, but Frank wasn't one to look a gift horse in the mouth.

Frank knew that Rainbow wouldn't approve. She didn't like him when he drank. He'd have to keep the stash of moonshine secret.

He grabbed a wooden tablespoon off the counter and dipped it into the jar. He lifted the spoon to his lips and took a sip.

"Whoa, that is powerful stuff," he stammered, his mouth puckering.

He poured a shot of moonshine into a measuring cup.

The dog ran into the room, a freshly killed rabbit in its mouth.

"Good boy, Blue," he said to the dog. "You keep those suckers away from the garden."

The dog dropped the rabbit's carcass at Frank's feet and woofed lightly.

"Down the hatch, buddy."

Frank downed the moonshine in one go. His eyes watered. His cheeks burned.

"Man, that is good hootch," he muttered, pouring himself a larger shot.

He counted the mason jars: one, two, three, four... eighteen in all. Frank danced a little jig, inadvertently stepping on the dog's paw. The dog yelped and scooted out of the way. Frank didn't notice.

"Thank you, Lady Providence, and thank you, Miss River, wherever you are in the Universe," he danced some more, and then downed the second shot.

"Woohoohoo," he hollered with glee.

The dog let out a low growl, picked up the dead rabbit, and raced across the yard to the house.

Too Bizarre for Words

"Have any ideas on where the lead poisoning may have come from, Bet," Forester asked Betty as he held the back door open for her.

There was just the two of them and the coroner's second in command, Jason, a strapping young man with a curly head of hair and a perpetual lost look on his face.

Corporal Singh had volunteered to stay behind and take Stew and Reggie's statements. God bless him, was all that Betty had said. It wasn't going to be a simple task with every man at the pub trying to register a complaint about the detective's electric trigger finger.

The last two techs from the party down at the beach sat outside in one of the panel vans doing the paperwork on the woman inside the body bag behind them. No clues as to her identity or where she had come from had turned up on the beach before the storm rolled in and made it impossible to continue the search.

Betty realized with a start that she was standing like an idiot in the doorway, arms at her sides, her mouth open in a round 'O', her equilibrium shattered by the sight of all the techs tearing through Andy's kitchen, taking food, water, juice, and wine samples from the open bottles. Every cupboard was open. Bags of flour, rice, and Quaker Oats were strewn across the countertops.

"What was I thinking," Forester stammered. "This must be terribly hard for you."

"I'm fine," Betty croaked, slipping off her boots and placing them on the boot mat by the door. "Let's get this done."

"Are you sure?"

"I'm sure."

"Anything yet, Sarah," Forester asked a dumpling faced girl in the kitchen.

"Not so far, but we haven't finished yet," the petite intern volunteered. "We checked the water from the tap first thing, but there were no signs of contaminants. It was the same results for the opened bottles of wine that we tested. That was only field-testing mind you, so maybe something will show up back at the lab."

Betty heard Powder and Hammerton's footsteps on the stairs.

The thought of the obnoxious detective sorting through Andy's personal items made Betty grimace. It ruffled her feathers enormously, but she kept quiet. It was his job. She didn't have to like it. It just miffed her it was being done by such an arrogant twit. She wistfully wished that she had brought Gertrude along for backup.

"Sergeant," Tom Powder's baritone voice echoed through the vast kitchen.

"Inspector," Betty replied, acknowledging him before switching her attention back to Doc Forester. "In answer to your question, Andy renovated the house about a year ago. I assume Andy had the contractor replace all the old copper piping, but I don't know for sure. He gutted the kitchen and dining room and took out a wall to make it all one big open space. My father could probably tell you more."

"Is there a crawlspace entrance where we can get under the house to check," Sarah asked.

"I honestly don't know," Betty shrugged helplessly. "I didn't spend that much time here. The original house had a dirt foundation. For all I know, it still does."

"That's not what we were told," the brash detective said, eyebrows raised.

"Hear-say, Inspector," Betty snapped without turning around, not wanting to talk about her personal relationship with Inspector Ben Hammerton, even though she knew she would have to at some point. "You should have learned that in basic training."

"Why don' we sit in the living room and go over what we know," Powder suggested.

Betty suspected that Powder was trying to avert World War Three. Good luck with that, she thought, squaring her shoulders.

"I don't know what I can tell you other than what is in my report," Betty grumbled, brushing past the two men.

"Do restrain your partner, Tom," Forester whispered into Powder's ear, "Betty is as good an officer as you and a close friend of mine."

"As best I can, Doc," Tom mumbled back.

***

The sun streaming through the living room windows brought a brief respite to the tension and gloominess in the house. The white walls in the living room exploded with light. The brightness was as blinding as a sun drenched day in the Arctic.

Sergeant Bruce took advantage of it, taking a seat, facing the room, the light from the bay window at her back creating a halo around her head, and shielding her face from scrutiny. Her cinnamon-colored hair flamed into life, a brilliant mix of gold, peaches and cream. The shadows in the places untouched by the sunlight were dark and foreboding.

Tom grinned as he took a seat across from Betty, knowing exactly what the Sergeant was doing. It was a brilliant tactical move, one that wasn't lost on either he or his partner.

Hammerton stood beside him rather than take a chair, casually taking a pair of dark sunglasses out of his suit pocket and putting them on.

This was going to be a painful interview.

"In your own words, I'd like to hear what happened when Mr. McDowell went over the cliff, and why you suspected him of murder," Tom asked, pulling a notebook from his pocket.

"And just how deep your relationship with the dead man was,"

Hammerton added.

Powder groaned inwardly, sure that Sergeant Bruce would spring from her chair and wipe the smirk right off his partner's face, but instead she sat quietly composed, hands in her lap, a stoic look on her face.

"It started when Gertrude went missing. Andy phoned and said that Peaches was missing too. Gertrude loved Eliza, so it seemed the logical place to start," Betty recounted her story, her voice strong and clear. "They especially enjoyed sharing tea."

"Figures it was the pig that started it all," Hammerton mumbled under his breath.

Betty glared at him, but then continued on unabated.

"I found Eliza floating upside down in her fish tank. A stool was knocked over and fish food was scattered about the floor. There was also a set of muddy gumboot prints, men's size 8 to be exact, on the floor. There was a slit on the underside of the right boot sole. Eliza was a neat freak, even had Gertie trained to stamp her feet on the floor mat at the front door before entering the house. If someone had visited her, why hadn't Eliza stopped to clean up the mud before feeding the fish? If Eliza was murdered and the tracks left at the scene were the killer's, then he'd be one of the dumbest sots in history. Gertrude may have run the killer off before he had time to cover his tracks, so to speak, but unlikely. Doc Forester declared Eliza's death an accidental death for want of any real evidence, but those damnable muddy boot prints bothered me."

"Interesting," Tom Powder said, scribbling more notes.

"I searched for a matching boot print among the mourners at Eliza's funeral, but didn't have any luck. Summer River tried to get Judge Bone's and my attention after the service, but she kept getting brushed aside. Andy, Stew Mann, the local pub owner, Barney Whyte, the chap who let you in here, Reggie Phoenix, a local fisherman, and my father, kept getting in her way. That wasn't that unusual given the sheer volume of people who attended the service. Eliza was a well loved. Vi, Judge Bone, Eliza's sister-in-law, finally managed to tell Summer that we'd pop by in a day or two. Unfortunately, other things got in the way and we were too late. We found Summer dead in the arms of a stone angel, having fallen from the barn roof."

"And again, that death was ruled accidental," Powder added.

"Yes. She was wearing a tool belt. She had been up the ladder trying to fix the lightning rod on top of the barn. There were some tools on the roof, and we could see where she had been tightening a bolt on the rod. She was in sandals. One of them must have caught on the ladder and she fell to her death."

"And you were at both scenes," Hammerton stated. "Interesting."

"Let her finish," Tom growled.

"You're right, Inspector, it was interesting. I found another set of gumboot tracks in the garden as well as a blackened mark on the metal plate the lightning rod was attached to," Betty stated. "It looked like a scorch mark, but we couldn't be sure when it happened, if it was from a lightning strike or if something else caused it. Doc found no signs of electrocution during the autopsy. She definitely died from the fall."

"Same odd circumstances as the first death then," Hammerton added, leaning forward.

"Yes. A couple of weeks later, Tiffany Hyde-White invited my dad and me to dinner. She intimated in her conversation with me I shouldn't trust Andy. She told me she had something she wanted to talk to me about but wanted to wait until she returned from a writer's conference in Hawaii."

"And low and behold, she died before she got to tell you what it was," Hammerton cut in. "Convenient."

"Will you let the Sergeant complete her report," Tom ordered his partner. "No more interruptions, Ben!"

The young man glowered but said nothing.

"Go on, please," Tom urged Betty.

"My father and I found her body in the garden and I called it in. Tiffany was allergic to peanuts. Everyone on the island knew it. She died because of a peanut laced chocolate," Betty said sadly. "And yes, there were gumboot tracks in the snow leading away from the scene."

"I understand that this lady had a bit of a reputation around here," Powder said, turning to his partner. He expected a wise crack, but Hammerton remained mute.

"Tiffany liked to party, but she was going to AA and was trying to turn her life around or, so I was told. I found that out from my ex-husband, Jim. He and Tiffany were seeing each other. They met at an AA meeting and fell in love. Tiffany wanted to tell dad and me about it at dinner. She didn't want us finding out about it through the island grape vine."

"Didn't he give her the chocolates?"

"He did, earlier in the day," Betty responded, looking towards the kitchen where Doc Forester and his techs were in deep discussion.

"He still lives with the guilt that it was him who gave Tiffany the chocolates but swears that the box of chocolates hadn't been tampered with," Betty added, switching her attention back to Powder and the interview.

"And you believe him," Hammerton asked quietly.

"I do. He's an ass, but Tiffany's death devastated him. He wasn't staying with Tiffany. He rented one of the oceanfront cottages down by the pub."

Betty paused for a moment, gathering her thoughts.

"Even I can see there is a pattern here, boss," Hammerton said to Tom Powder, his posture softening.

Tom nodded, more to himself than his partner. There was more to the story than what was in the official report.

"After that, Vi and I decided that we would do some more investigating on our own. Until we found out who the gumboot tracks belonged to, we weren't going to let it go. It wasn't until Andy threatened Vi at the wharf that everything went south. Vi found an incriminating email on Eliza's computer regarding Andy and Tiffany's writing relationship. The email was from Tiffany. She told Eliza that she was afraid of him. We didn't know Tiffany was talking about Andy. Vi had also found out that Summer filed a paternity suit against him. The suit was settled out of court. It cost Andy a bundle. That was when he became our prime suspect."

Betty inhaled sharply. Beads of sweat coated her brow. She rubbed her trembling hands together and let out her breath slowly.

"Andy confessed to killing Eliza, Summer and Tiffany. Up to that point, we had assumed Summer's death was accidental and couldn't figure out why he would kill her when the paternity suit was already over. The more I think about it, the more it remains a puzzle."

The Sergeant looked Powder in the eye, her gaze was unwavering.

"Tiffany was a whole different story. Tiffany ghost wrote Andy's bestselling romances. Only their agent knew. The two of them split the proceeds. Andy said he got sixty percent and Tiffany took forty percent of the royalties. They didn't want the truth getting out because it would kill their sales. The publishing company played up Andy's lady-killer looks and charm. Women fell all over him at book signings. He told me about it. The media frenzy probably would have ended both of their careers."

"Kind of like that Millie Vanillie scandal back in its day," Hammerton nodded with understanding.

"Yes, just like that."

"So were the gumboots at the murder scenes his then," Hammerton asked, sitting down on the couch.

Powder could see that his partner was as intrigued by the Sergeant's accounts as he was himself.

"No. They were my father's," Betty confessed, her shoulders slumping. "He and Eliza became close after Wally and my mom died. He was over at Eliza's that morning. She gave him some muffins to bring home. They wanted to tell me about their relationship over lunch later that day."

"But that never happened," Powder commented dryly.

"No, that never happened," Betty agreed. "As for Summer, Dad visited her all the time. Summer was like a second daughter to him. I wasn't here very much, and Summer was all alone, both her parents, and her fiancé, were gone. You must understand that this is a small island. Everyone looks after everyone here."

"Except when they're killing each other," Hammerton quipped.

Powder let the comment ride. He silently agreed with his partner.

"And what about Ms. Hyde-White," Hammerton asked. "What was your father's relationship with her?"

Powder sighed in defeat and scribbled more notes in his notebook. He looked up in time to see the Sergeant wince.

"They were just friends," Betty croaked.

Powder knew she was covering something up. It obviously involved her father.

"So, you considered your father a prime suspect too," Hammerton stated matter-of-factly.

"Yes, at one point."

"And you were intimately involved with Andy McDowell," Tom added.

"Yes."

Hammerton and Powder exchanged a knowing glance.

"And with that, I'll leave you two capable detectives to sort it all out. I'm exhausted and I have a dead woman and a severed foot to deal with. You know where to find me," Betty stated, standing up.

"You still haven't told us exactly what happened in your boyfriend's last moments," Hammerton commented dryly.

"He tried to kill me, my father, and Judge Bone. Dad and I caught him red handed, trying to throw the Judge off the cliff. He was in a rage. He broke my father's ribs. I'd never seen him like that before, wouldn't even have thought it possible. I'm ashamed to say that he got the better of me. Gertrude saved our lives. She pushed him off the cliff. If you need to know anything else, talk to Judge Bone."

Betty brushed a tear from her eye. She spun around and strode past the two men, her back rigid and jaw set.

Tom and his partner followed her into the kitchen.

"I'll talk to you later about our floater, Doc," Betty said stopping to slip on her gumboots.

"You mean floaters," the coroner said good-naturedly as Betty slid open the patio door.

"Yeah, floaters," Betty mumbled, closing the patio doors behind her.

"So, what do you think," Powder asked Hammerton, after the Sergeant had left.

Tom's partner was brash, impulsive, and insensitive, but he was an astute detective who had a gift for piecing together the most difficult of cases.

"I think the Sergeant is right. I think the women were murdered. I also think we still may find that the boyfriend did it, despite him being high on LSD and suffering from lead poisoning. He had a motive in all three deaths, but so did the Sergeant's father and I hate to say this, but you did see what the Sergeant was wearing on her feet."

"Yeah, gumboots," Powder replied thoughtfully.

"Big question is why did the hippie chic accuse our dead guy of being the father of her unborn baby? Did she honestly think it was him? From what our files say, she was loaded herself, so money wasn't a reason. Also, why didn't McDowell have a DNA test done? Why pay the hippie chic a million bucks to go away if he didn't have to? The whole case is one giant question mark," Ben growled.

Tom agreed. The whole case was one big conundrum.

"And another thing," Hammerton grimaced. "How come they didn't turn that pig into bacon? I mean, if a dog kills somebody, they put it down. Am I right or am I right?"

"I suggest you don't go saying that to anyone else but me," Tom urged his partner.

"Just saying, this island is one messed up place."

"You can say that again," Powder agreed.

A shadow flitted across the side window, heading towards the front of the house.

The Inspector and his partner walked back into the living

room.

Powder waited for Ben to continue, but it seemed the junior detective was all talked out.

The two men watched through the living room window as Betty strode around the front of the house, gumboots and lumberjack jacket flapping, hands in her pockets, the angular lines of her expression at odds with the roundness of her face.

Powder felt a stab of pity for the woman.

No Bones About It

Violet Bone sat in her favorite Lazy boy chair in front of the fireplace. The gold corduroy material was worn, and the frame slumped in the middle, but Vi didn't care. It was the warmest spot in the old house. The crackling flames from the fire reflected in her grey eyes.

It had been a cold and drafty winter, even here in northern California in the gabled house on the beach that she had bought years ago as a winter vacation home.

The minute she returned to Vancouver from Seal Island, she knew she just had to get away from it all... from the city... the province... and even the country. This seemed like the perfect place.

The colorful shawl that her deceased sister-in-law, Eliza, had knitted for her many years ago was wrapped around Vi's petite form. Her tiny feet tapped out the beat of the old Sinatra tune playing on the radio. She didn't realize she was doing it, so lost in thought a bear rampaging through the living room wouldn't have disturbed her.

One arthritic hand rested on top of a dog-eared paperback novel. The book's title was *The Dastardly Mister Deeds*. She propped the other hand under her chin.

The book had given her pause.

It was a strange tale written by Tiffany Hyde-White, President of the Seal Island Vagabond Writer's Society up until her untimely death several months earlier. The Writer's Society was defunct, having lost three of its charter members in a most unsettling way.

She drummed her fingers atop the cover of the book.

Tiffany had solved the mystery of the severed feet in sneakers that had washed up on the beaches of British Columbia and Puget Sound in a most peculiar way, one that as bizarre as the story was, had a ring of truth to it. Tiffany's dark and twisted tale reminded Vi of a case she had read about somewhere, but she couldn't quite put her finger on it. The memory was buried deep inside the clutter of her mind. Like a loose thread in a silk scarf, if she tugged at it long enough, Vi knew that the memory would unwind.

The retired judge sighed.

She hadn't spoken to Betty or her father since she left the island two weeks ago. Those two weeks were a blur of pain and anguish.

Vi felt like she had let Eliza down.

Her soul ached with defeat.

How could she ever go back there?

Yet even still, she missed Seal Island and its crazy occupants, the view of Vancouver Island from Wally and Eliza's back porch, cuddling with that rascal of a pig, Gertrude, and dinner at the pub. Oh, how she loved Stew's burgers.

Her stomach growled in response.

The shrill ring of the phone startled the cat. Percival jumped up and dashed away from his comfy perch by the fire. The beautiful grey Persian had adjusted well to life with her; although, she knew by his twitching tail and vacant stares out the window that he occasionally missed life on the farm with Summer River.

The name on the telephone's call display made her heart quicken. She didn't know whether to laugh or cry.

"Betty, I was just thinking about you," Vi said, her voice strong and clear as she answered the phone.

"I'm afraid this isn't really a social call," Betty confessed. "I wanted to respect your privacy, what with everything that happened and your listing of the house for sale, but I wanted to give you a heads up in case you weren't notified about what's going on up here."

"You mean the results of Andy's autopsy," Vi queried, a frown creasing her forehead.

"Ah, so Doc Forester called you then."

"I asked him to email me a copy of the results when they were ready. He was kind enough to do so. I take it he and his lab techs found what they were looking for at Andy's house?"

"No, they haven't found the cause of the lead poisoning as far as I know, and no one has said anything to me about finding any LSD either."

"I must say that Andy never struck me as the LSD type, but for all we knew, he may have used it for inspiration. He told me that Tiffany didn't write all of his books," Vi replied with a shudder. She pulled the shawl tightly around her light frame.

"Huh, that's interesting. Anyway, I wanted to let you know that you may get a call from Inspector Tom Powder or his partner, Ben Hammerton, if you haven't already. Powder is an okay guy, but that Hammerton is a piece of work."

"No, not a peep, but only a few people have my number down here. Obviously, you are no longer working the case?"

"Not that one. It's a good thing I guess since Gertie found another severed foot. It's been all over the news channels."

"Good heavens, on Seal Island?"

"Close to the landing," Betty confided. "Plus, Reggie and Stew found a floater that I still haven't been able to identify."

Vi gasped.

And here she was just thinking about how much she missed the lazy lifestyle of the island.

"Sorry, I didn't mean to burden you with all of this," Betty stammered.

"Don't worry, my dear. I'm still not over what happened, but maybe a short visit to the island will help me find some closure."

"It would be lovely to see you again and I know my dad misses your company."

Violet smiled sadly. She liked Archie. Archie and Eliza would have made a lovely couple.

"I hope you can wait to return until I'm back on the island. I'm in Vancouver right now. I have to resolve this new case first plus see what I can come up with on these darn severed feet," Betty added.

"You know Betty, maybe I'm just a dotty old judge who needs to hang up her crime fighting cape, but I think you should pick up a copy of Tiffany's book, *The Dastardly Mister Deeds*. It is a bizarre story. I can't put my finger on it, but something about how she solves the mystery of the dismembered feet has a ring of truth in it," Vi suggested, staring absently at the burning logs in the fireplace once more. "Then again I'm getting a little long in the tooth to be playing at detective."

Betty laughed aloud.

"Well, here's a kicker for you," Betty continued, her voice lighter than it was before. "Andy left me his house and all its contents in his Will. I am quite sure he has copies of all of Tiffany's books in his library. I'll look when I get back."

"Oh, my, that is a kicker as you so quaintly put it." Vi grinned. She knew the handsome rogue loved Betty, even with everything that had transpired. She forgave him, at least a little bit.

"Do pickup a copy of that book, after all Tiffany's Detective Mazie Owen is based on you don't forget! And please don't step on either of those detective's toes you mentioned."

On the other end of the line, Betty laughed.

"I'll try not to. Take care, Vi. Let me know when you're coming to the island and I'll make a point of being there," Betty finished.

Vi hung up the phone.

That was an interesting call.

Maybe she wasn't too old after all. Maybe she would put her sleuthing hat back on. Maybe Eliza could finally rest in peace and so could she.

***

Betty sat back in her chair. Her conversation with Vi was illuminating. Neither Tom Powder nor the Nordic God he worked with had bothered to call the Judge. That was either good or bad news, depending on how she looked at it.

If she wasn't so busy, she might have called Inspector Powder to ask how the investigation was going, but she also knew that Vi wouldn't approve, nor would her boss. It wasn't a good time to do it, anyway. She was tired and more than a little cranky.

"Hey, Bet, you'll never guess what," the Duty Sergeant called out to her from the break room.

Betty grabbed her empty coffee cup and wandered past the several cubicles between hers and the small kitchen.

"W'as up, Benny," she asked Sergeant Kim.

"Some clown was in this morning filing a missing person report on his wife," Kim said, a steaming cup of mint tea in his hands.

"She run away from the circus with a lion tamer or something," Betty quipped.

"That's what I asked him? He didn't think it was very funny," the wiry raven-haired sergeant added. "Seriously, he was the real deal, complete with a tiny black clown hat, a big red nose, grease paint, and a water squirting flower in his lapel."

"No kidding," Betty said, brushing by Kim.

"Clown's name was Roy Everett. The description of his wife sounded like it might be your floater. Five foot six, auburn hair, twenty-four years of age and flashy nails, he said. It was the flashy nail comment that struck me as odd."

"Odd compared to what, a clown walking into a cop station? That sounds like it might be our floater, though. What else did he say," she asked Kim.

"He said he and the missus were out on their boat. They had been drinking and had a fight. Maybe it was about the lion tamer?" Kim laughed. "Anyway, she stormed off into the cabin and locked the main hatch. He passed out in the cockpit. He said he was drinking pretty heavy all the way up the coast to Prince Rupert. It wasn't until he pulled into port and came back to the boat with an Egg McMuffin for her that he found the boat hatch was no longer locked and his wife was gone. There's a scanned picture of her in the file. I emailed it to you."

"And he didn't report her missing until two weeks later," Betty asked, incredulous.

"What can I say? Clown of the year, I guess. Anyway, the boat's name is the *Just in Time*. It's a 1999 thirty-foot Ciera Bayliner, originally registered in the States. The clown's cell number is in the file. The boat is docked at Gibsons."

"Thanks, Benny," she said, pouring herself a fresh cup of java. Betty thought it smelled divine, even if it was some no-name brand. That was when her tiredness really hit her.

Still, it sounded like Benny's clown might be the break in the case she was looking for. That poor girl deserved better than to end up with her remains unidentified and nobody missing her. There was nothing worse than a file winding up a cold case.

Betty returned to her desk.

Betty pulled up the internal RCMP database on her computer and typed in the link that Benny had emailed to her.

She sipped her coffee and read the report. Sure enough, it was just like Benny said: booze, fight, missing woman, all in that order.

Betty pulled up the picture of Sarah Everett, a bikini-clad fun-loving young twenty-something with sparkling brown eyes, auburn hair, and glittery nails. She hammed it up for the camera, her goofy grin and carefree spirit shining through. The lovely Sarah Everett now lay on a cold steel table in the morgue; she was definitely Betty's floater.

Betty got a team together right away to visit Mr. Roy Everett, aka The Clown, at the docks instead of calling him in to the precinct. Maybe she could get him to confess to the murder at the scene of the crime, or at least be able to determine if there was a murder at all?

She tried hard not to let the happenings on Seal Island affect her view of her active cases, but it was getting increasingly hard not to see murder and mayhem at every turn.

Betty rubbed her eyes. A migraine was forming behind her eyeballs. Any minute now, the band would start up, complete with crashing cymbals and kettle drums.

It seemed almost fitting that Sarah Everett had washed up on Seal Island's rocky shores.

***

A complex unit of steel drums, copper piping, and glass tubing took up most of Barney's metal shed on his property on Seal Island.

Wood heated the main drum in which the corn mash mixture was distilled. It was a huge still, almost industrial. On the floor in one corner lay sacks of corn, barley and rye, along with jugs of spring water. Nestled between the sacks of corn and barley was a basket of navel oranges. Two yellow lemons added to the colorful array. A cord of neatly stacked split oak, cedar and fir, lined the doorway.

Several rows of moonshine filled mason jars sat on the earthen floor, regimentally straight, backs against the far wall. A plastic milk crate filled with steam cleaned empty glass milk bottles sat on a bench. Stenciled on the side of the milk bottles was "Barney's Brew".

Barney, buck naked and humming, picked up a small tin of pipe tobacco and spun open the top. Inside the tin was a pile of little orange pills with a red smiley face stamped on the top. He poured out a handful of pills and grinned elfishly. He put one pill inside two of the empty milk bottles and then doubled up the pills in a few others.

His task accomplished, he did a little jig, picked up an empty shot glass and then opened the spigot on the capture tank. He plopped one of the little orange pills into the shot of warm liquid that filled the glass.

He downed the shot in one gulp, smacking his lips together as he did so.

"Gonna take a little trip on a magic carpet ride," he sang gleefully.

The old man grabbed a mason jar filled with moonshine, and then raced out of the shed, across the yard, and around the side patio, his penis swinging from side to side like a rubbery pendulum, his bare feet slapping on the patio stones.

He zigzagged through the garden and past the stone angel that he had removed from Summer's farm and placed beside the walkway that led down to the beach where his beautiful wife waited for him inside a steaming hot tub. The angel's open arms reached for the sky, its stony face beatific, and its eyes unwilling to reveal the ugly truth of what it had last held upraised in offering.

Camille swirled the merlot in her wine glass around and around, mesmerized by the sound of the waves crashing on the rocks below the hot tub's raised platform. Her ample breasts peaked above the water line. She smiled for no other reason than she was content. Steam from the hot tub tickled her nostrils.

She let her mind drift away, the alcohol and hot water lulling her senses, until her husband leapt into the tub with a loud splash. Water cascaded over the sides of the hot tub as he made his way towards her, the hand holding his moonshine held high above his head.

Camille laughed and wrapped her long legs around him, drawing him towards her.

"Is that a banana is your pants," she drawled.

"It would be if I was wearing any," he drawled back.

Camille's eyes sparkled as her husband pulled her close. For a man his age, he was in marvelous shape and had the endurance of a young bull.

"What's that in your hand," she cooed.

Barney plopped a hit of LSD into her wine glass.

"Drink up, my dear, time to party," he whispered huskily.

Camille grinned. She downed the wine and then turned around, leaning back into Barney's broad chest.

"You always knew how to keep a girl amused," she gasped as he folded his sturdy arms around her.

"As do you my love," he crooned softly, nibbling on her ear.

"Hmmmm, you are such a devil."

"You don't know the half of it."

"I was thinking…," she murmured, looking up into his steely eyes.

"That's a dangerous thing," he joked.

"We should buy Bone's Bailiwick."

"Why would we do that," Barney grunted.

"No reason. I just thought it might be a magnificent conversation piece."

"A conversation piece," he asked, puzzled.

"Well, how often do you get to purchase a bonafide murder house, and not some stuffy Civil War mansion either, but a quaint little cottage by the sea where the owner drowned in her fish tank," Camille cooed.

"Well," he said, his voice deepening with desire, "that would be a good conversation piece except we really don't know if our friend, Eliza, was murdered or not, do we?"

"Don't we," Camille replied softly, spinning around and grabbing her husband in a vise like grip.

"Is there something that you're not telling me, my love," Barney asked huskily.

"Oooohhhh, I thought maybe there was something you weren't telling me," she quipped before playfully catching her husband's lower lip between her teeth.

"My God, but you are beautiful," he whispered, pulling away.

Camille purred with delight.

"Why not Tiffany's place," he asked quietly. "After all, she died by chocolate in the garden with her gnomes."

"Too vulgar. It sounds like one of those board game murder mystery thingies. Besides, I never liked her," Camille answered.

"And you liked Eliza," he asked her.

"More or less," Camille purred, pulling the hand holding the glass of moonshine towards her. She took a sip. "Wowsers, but that has a kick to it?"

"It's a manly-man drink."

"Prove it!"

Barney laughed and then kissed his wife passionately.

Roy the Clown & The Painted Lady

"Hello, on board," Betty yelled from the dock at Gibson's Landing. She signaled the four officers who had accompanied her to fan out along the dock, in case the clown tried to bolt, either by foot or by boat. If by boat, he wouldn't get far. The RCMP naval unit was moored on the far side of the harbor, ready for action.

The forensic crew, including Doc Forester, waited at the foot of the dock.

The *Just in Time* wasn't a poor man's boat, but it wasn't a millionaire's either. She was thirty feet of sleek fiberglass with a covered upper cockpit and a lower cabin. Betty had looked up the boat's specs on-line.

A short, balding bleary-eyed fifty-year-old unzipped the canopy door in the cockpit and peeked out. Santa Claus cheeks and a bulbous red nose spoke to his drinking habits, but the sparkling brown eyes that regarded her were warm and inviting. He had removed most of his face paint, but Betty could still see the faint outlines of black triangles around his eyes and a wide red mouthed clown smiley face. Roy Everett was not what she expected.

"Can I help you," he asked politely.

Roy Everett was older than his wife. He was at least twice her age. Betty grimaced: she had worried about the ten years difference between Andy and her.

Roy was grey at the temples and his face was round, his body portly, and his legs bow-legged. His goatee was white and in need of a trim, but other than that, he was a plain looking man with a pleasant disposition.

"My name's Sergeant Betty Bruce. I'm with the RCMP Major Crimes Investigation Unit. I'd like to come aboard and talk to you about your wife, Sarah," she said evenly, relaxing her stance. Roy Everett reminded her of Reggie Phoenix for some reason.

"Major crimes? But I just reported Sarah missing this morning," he answered, confused.

"That's what I need to talk to you about," she replied softly. "Can I come aboard?"

"Yeah, come on," he waved her forward. "Can I get you a coffee?"

"No thanks. I'm coffee'd out right now."

Betty signaled for her men to watch her back and the forensics team to stay where they were.

Betty stepped down onto the deck, found her balance, and then made her way up the couple of steps to the upper cockpit where a soulful eyed Roy Everett sat down in the captain's chair, a steaming mug of coffee in his hands.

She idly looked around. A bottle of Bailey's Irish Cream rested beside several empty pizza boxes on the deck beneath the white leather captain's chair. The sleek lines of the cockpit were spotless; the chrome instrument panel spit polished to a high sheen. That didn't bode well for forensics.

"Take a seat," Everett said, motioning her to the mate's chair.

"Thanks, I'll stand," Betty replied. While her inner senses told her this man was harmless, her cop's training made her wary.

The cockpit awning hid the officers from Everett's view, but it also made it difficult for Betty to see them as well which made her uncomfortable. It was a rookie mistake.

"So, what has Sarah done this time," he asked dejectedly.

"Why would you ask that," Betty queried.

"With my lovely wife's record," he responded with a look of incredulity on his face.

Betty bit her lip. She hadn't thought to run Sarah Everett's name through the system. Clearly, she was off her game. Maybe, she needed to go home for a while.

Roy sighed heavily.

"Look, Sarah does this all the time. When she gets pissed at me, she cleans out our joint account and goes to the casino. I went to pick up breakfast in Port Hardy and came back to the boat to surprise her, only to find that she was gone. I was upset, but not worried. I figured she hitched a ride to the nearest airport and took a plane back to Vancouver. When I got back, expecting to find her at home, she wasn't there. She wasn't at her favorite casino either. She always comes home after a few days, but when she didn't, I checked her accounts and discovered she hadn't touched them. That's when I got really worried and filed a missing person report. Now Major Crimes shows up on my boat, so I figure she got herself into a mess at the casino."

"That's why it took you two weeks to report Sarah missing," Betty countered, staring down at him.

"Look, I know what you think, fat middle aged geezer who likes to dress up as a clown and a pretty young wife. I guarantee you Sarah didn't run away with a lion tamer or circus strong man. That joke got old fast. I didn't chase Sarah. She chased me. I love life. I love to travel and was lucky enough to do okay for myself and retire early. Sarah and I wanted the same things. I love her more than anything else in his world. I give her whatever she wants, mostly money for fancy nail jobs and an hour or two at the slots. She loves her painted claws. That's what she calls them, 'painted claws'. I thought it was so darned cute. So, tell me, why are you here?"

Betty looked down into his earnest face.

"Where is Sarah," Roy asked, his face suddenly ashen. "Has something happened to her? She didn't get into some trouble with a bookie or anything, did she?"

Betty choked on her words. It wasn't that long ago that she had lost someone she cared about too.

The clown sensed the answer.

Tears formed in Roy Everett's eyes.

"I'm sorry, Roy. Sarah's dead," Betty replied gently, finally finding her voice. "Her body washed up on Seal Island two weeks ago."

For the first time in his life, Roy Everett had nothing to say. Instead, he crumpled, his entire body shaking with violent tremors.

Betty tried to grab him before he crashed to the ground, but he was too heavy. Her face bounced off the back of the captain's chair.

A deep wail of grief erupted from the broken-hearted man.

Betty helped him into a sitting position. She wondered if Roy the Clown would ever perform at the Children's Hospital again.

Betty heard a series of heavy footsteps on the dock.

She placed a comforting hand on the stricken man's shoulder as her team vaulted onto the boat, weapons drawn. She motioned for them to stand down.

Her team members holstered their weapons and then helped Roy to his feet. He stood shakily, an officer holding him up by each arm. He was shaking so bad that they almost had to carry him off the boat. One of her officers ran to his cruiser and brought back a blanket which he then tenderly draped over Roy the Clown's shoulders.

Betty donned a pair of latex gloves and waited patiently for Doc Forester and his team to arrive. Hopefully, they could shed some light on what had happened to Sarah Everett. Maybe the knowing would not only put Sarah's husband's fears to rest, but Betty's own. Maybe Roy the Clown would get his smile back one day.

***

"Ouch, that's gonna leave a shiner," Doc Forester said, seeing Betty's dark rimmed eye.

Betty gingerly fingered her right eye.

"Yeah, I expect so," she grumbled.

"The things you do in the line of service," the coroner sympathized, handing her an ice pack.

Betty accepted the ice pack. She placed it on her sore eye. She sighed with relief, the coldness relieving the throbbing around her eye socket.

The forensic crew spread out over the boat like spiders, inside the cabin, the cockpit, and across the deck.

"Hello, *Just in Time*," a familiar voice called from the dock.

Betty squinted down at the man standing on the dock.

"Inspector Powder, what are you doing here," she asked politely.

"Guess I should have been here earlier. I missed all the fun," Powder grinned. "I hear you caught a clown fish."

"Nothing was caught, but a broken man. It wasn't any fun either," Betty grimaced.

"How about I buy you a steak for that eye and a hamburger for lunch?"

"Got some blood and hair over here," one of the forensic techs yelled to the coroner before Betty could answer.

Doc Forester strode across the deck. He examined the dried blood and hair follicles on the railing. There were also a few tiny pieces of shattered glass stuck inside a deck molding. One shard was thin and cylindrical.

"Maybe a shattered wine glass," Doc Forester said, pointing towards the glass shards. "Bag and tag it. Good work, Jason."

"You figure this is where your floater came from, Sergeant," Powder asked quietly.

"Yeah, husband's distraught," she replied.

Doc Forester pulled a set of tweezers from his bag and gathered up the hair.

"Definitely same color as our painted lady," Forester added, putting the long strands of hair in a bag and handing it to his technician.

"Painted lady," Powder inquired.

"Victim had unicorns and rainbows painted on her nails," Betty answered wearily. She gingerly felt her eye. It was continuing to swell. "Husband's a clown."

"So, I heard."

"He volunteers at the Children's Hospital."

"Why don't you go get that steak and hamburger with the

Inspector," Forester encouraged her. "I'll call you with my report. We'll be here for a while."

"Can't argue with the doc," Powder replied cheerily.

"Yeah, okay," she said.

The deck canted sideways when Betty stepped off the ladder and onto the stern deck. She reeled backwards. Powder wrapped an arm around her waist before she tottered overboard.

"Thanks," she mumbled, embarrassed.

"That happens sometimes when you've only got one good eye," he advised her. "Shiners can really screw up the equilibrium."

"Hardy-har-har, me matey," she growled in her best pirate voice.

Powder burst out laughing.

The techs on the boat grinned.

"Take care of my girl, Inspector," Forester waved from the starboard side of the *Just In Time*.

"Aye, aye, Captain."

***

Betty and Tom sat at a corner table in a White Spot restaurant.

The waitress who served them was timid, eyeing Betty's eye like she didn't know whether to ask her if she was all right, call the cops, or go on break until they left. Her hands shook as she poured the coffee.

"He did it," Betty joked, nodding towards Tom Powder. "He's got a killer right hook."

"Left actually," he replied amiably.

The waitress bolted.

"I think we just terrified her," Powder said, watching the woman disappear into the manager's office.

"Better not pull out our guns then," Betty chuckled. She took a sip of coffee.

They sat in silence for a moment.

"You think the clown killed the painted lady," Powder asked, opening the menu.

Betty glanced sideways at the Inspector. The dark brown eyes that regarded her were shrewd and intelligent. Powder carried himself with ease. He seemed a peaceful man. She was grateful that he had agreed to review the Seal Island cases.

"I honestly don't know. My gut tells me that he didn't. He was genuinely distraught at hearing of her death. It sounded like they loved each other very much despite their age difference. It may well be that our painted lady took a fall, bumped her head, and fell into the strait. Hubby was too drunk to hear her cries for help and she drowned. It's a sad end to a young life."

Powder sipped his coffee.

Betty sipped hers.

The waitress didn't return.

"I was going to buy you lunch," Powder said, signaling another server. This server looked as terrified as the first one and bolted for the kitchen.

"I think we may have to find a drive-thru," Betty mused. "I should have worn my uniform. I usually do, I just didn't want to spook Roy."

"Huh, wonder why," Powder chortled.

Betty laughed and then winced. Her eye was killing her. She was afraid to look in the mirror.

"So, changing the subject, what's up with your investigation," she asked idly.

"Well, we're not any farther ahead than you were," Tom answered honestly. "These deaths appear to be tragic accidents. There is nothing that Doc Forester could find showing otherwise, even after going over all the evidence again. I haven't spoken to Judge Bone or your father yet, but I will."

"You can talk to my father anytime. I know the Judge will let you in the cottage at any time, but the aquarium is gone and Vi had the cottage scrubbed from top to bottom after Eliza died. Reggie took the Oscars, even promised at Eliza's funeral not to eat them."

Powder snorted.

"Tiffany's place is up for sale. I expect it was professionally cleaned so that won't help you either. Ditto for the cottage Jim rented. The McDonalds have moved into Summer River's place so that's a dead end."

"Kind of what I expected. All we really have is the original evidence and photos," Tom conceded. "And your boyfriend's confession."

"Which can't be believed," Betty stated matter-of-factly.

"Which can't be believed," the Inspector agreed.

"Did you find the source of the lead poisoning or LSD," Betty asked, finishing her coffee.

"The doc thinks the lead poisoning might be from prolonged exposure. He thinks lead contaminated the old pipes, but they're long gone so he can't prove it."

"I suppose that's a relief since I may end up moving in to the house. What about the drugs?"

"Nothing in the house; however, a friend of mine works Vice and he told me that there has been a lot of acid and a real lethal angel dust cocktail hitting the streets lately. He seems to think the LSD may come from the same lab. Know of anyone from the Island who might have those kinds of connections?"

"Not a clue," Betty said, totally puzzled.

"What about that pot grower, Reggie Phoenix," Powder asked. "Think he may have moved up in the world?"

"Nah, Reg likes weed and beer. He's harmless. He wouldn't touch that kind of thing."

"You sure?"

"Positive," Betty said. "I can ask him if he knows anything about it though. He'll tell me. I've known Reg forever. I was thinking of asking him to take me out on his trawler to look at tidal patterns in the area and see if he has any ideas of where that foot that Gertie found may have come from."

"Ah, the shoe that fits the other foot and the search for the bodies that belong to the severed feet," Tom acknowledged. "How's that investigation going?"

"The foot was sawed off. Bones didn't break at the joint like on a floater the fish got to first; at least, not this one. Some of them are different; some are the same. Four of them don't have saw marks. Some are female and some are male. The feet were removed after death."

"It truly is a mystery."

"I want to trace the tidal patterns in the area to see if we can figure out where they all came from. Was it one place or different places? We had the Coast Guard experts in, but they weren't much help. We've got nine feet so far, all found in various locations up and down the coast."

"And you think your buddy the pot-head can help," Powder said with little conviction.

"He's not a pot-head. He's a retired fisherman who has a medical license to grow pot. And, yes, I think he knows more about the coastal waters around Seal Island than any of the boys at the Coast Guard. Besides, he successfully grew pot on the coast for years without getting caught," Betty laughed. "Who better to ask?"

"That's true," Tom concluded.

Tom looked around. There was still no service, and he was hungry.

"Well, now that we've covered our cases and I still haven't been able to buy you a steak or a hamburger, I suggest we pay for our coffee and go find a drive thru," Tom muttered.

"Excellent idea," Betty agreed, standing up.

They heard a commotion behind them as a sea of police cars pulled up front, sirens blaring, lights flashing.

"What do you think is going on," Powder asked innocently as he saw the manager escorting customers out the back door of the restaurant.

"I think you're about to get arrested," Betty said, raising her hands in the air as she looked across the restaurant into a dozen gun barrels.

"Sure, blame it on the Indian," Powder quipped, raising his hands.

"On the ground," a Swat team member shouted.

"We're cops," Betty shouted back.

"Whatever you do, don't try for your badge," Tom advised her. "You look like a crook to me."

"Thanks a lot."

"GUN," another Swat member screamed.

"That's guns, plural, and badges," Powder screamed. "Inspector Tom Powder, RCMP Major Crimes Investigation Unit."

"Sergeant Bruce, RCMP Major Crimes Investigation Unit."

The two of them were strong armed to the floor.

"Damn city police," Powder growled.

***

Betty threw her keys on the kitchen table as she entered her apartment and plunked a brown paper bag with a bottle of dry red wine and a dog-eared paperback inside on the table. She wasn't much of a drinker, but tonight she planned on settling down with a full glass of wine beside her and a book in her lap. To say the day had been both interesting and exhausting was an understatement.

Roy the Clown identified Sarah the Painted Lady in the morgue. Doc Forester was prepared to rule the death accidental. Roy the Clown wasn't a killer clown like in Stephen King's story; *It.* Roy was as much a victim of his wife's drowning as his wife was.

Betty rummaged through a kitchen drawer looking for a corkscrew. The skin around her eye was now varying shades of black, purple, blue and yellow.

She finally found a battered old wooden corkscrew and pulled a wineglass down from the cupboard, blowing the dust out of it as she did so.

She uncorked the Merlot, poured herself a giant glass of it, snatched Tiffany's book off the table, and then headed for the bedroom.

Betty stripped off her uniform and climbed into bed.

"So, Miss Tiffany, let's see how much your Detective Mazie

Owen resembles me and how you solved the case of the severed feet," she muttered as she tucked herself into bed and opened the copy of *The Dastardly Mr Deeds.* She had to go to five used bookstores to find this battered copy, the mainstream bookstores telling her they just couldn't keep it in stock since Tiffany's tragic death. The clerks suggested she download an e-book and thought her strange when she told them she didn't own an e-reader. It wasn't from any prejudice against them, she simply didn't have enough hours in the day.

Outside her apartment windows, the storm that had threatened the coast all day opened and unleashed a violent sluice of rain upon the city.

The Dastardly Mr. Deeds

By Tiffany Hyde Whyte

Detective Mazie Owen was broad of shoulder and hip, but not of humor. Her cinnamon-colored hair framed a deeply tanned face, her gaze fixed upon the photos of the severed feet in sneakers that were lined up on the table in front of her.

She turned a page of the Coroner's Report on the two latest discoveries, one a man's size nine and the other a lady's size six, her face darkening as she read the Coroner's findings.

Unlike the last six severed feet, which had already been reduced to bone inside the worn sneakers, the two recently found feet still had flesh on them. The bones were cleanly sawed off at the ankles and the flesh showed signs of formaldehyde, glutaraldehyde, ethanol, and humectants, which meant that the body to which the feet were attached had been embalmed before entering the water.

That put a whole new spin on her team's investigation.

Finally, a break!

Mazie pushed the Coroner's Report aside and popped open her laptop. She pulled up the tidal charts for the Gulf Islands. She googled all the funeral homes and cemeteries on the islands and then overlapped her pin chart of the locations in which they found the severed feet.

She pulled out her notepad and wrote down the addresses and contact information for the two cemeteries and one funeral home that interconnected on all three maps. These were the Angel's Gate Funeral Home and the Pearly Everlasting Funeral Home and Crematorium.

She tapped her pen against the notebook.

The Angel's Gate Funeral Home struck a bell. There was something *about the name.*

She opened the search button on the city's police database and typed in the name. Immediately, a case file came up.

Bernie Castleman, the previous owner of Angel's Gate, was doing fifteen years in a medium security prison for fraud. Bernie had been selling tainted tissue off corpses to transplant companies. Luckily, no one had died. The charges were reduced from attempted murder to fraud and tampering with a dead body along with several other miscellaneous charges after Castleman agreed to a guilty plea.

A grim smile creased her round face, the worry lines around her eyes deepening.

"Angel's Gate Funeral Home, Mr Marvin Deeds, Manager and Sole Proprietor," Mazie purred. "I think you and I need to have a talk."

***

Detective Owen drove off the small ferry onto Jebediah Island. She drove her own vehicle, a twenty-year-old SUV with rust in the quarter panels and a dented rear bumper.

Mazie wore a simple pale blue sweater that matched the color of her eyes and black slacks. She wanted to get a 'feel' for Mr Marvin Deeds, without the tight-lipped guarded response that a police uniform would garner.

Mazie had also come alone.

If she was right, and the tingling on the back of her neck told her she was bang-on, then Angel's Gate Funeral Home just might be the answer to the mystery that had tormented her investigative team for six years.

It wasn't that Mazie wanted all the glory for herself, but if her intuition was wrong, she didn't want to look like a fool in front of the men and women she worked with every day.

She told herself that this was a fact-finding mission and nothing more.

Mazie drove her old Ford Bronco up the narrow winding road dotted with hobby farms and artist galleries to the far side of the island where Angel's Gate Funeral Home was situated on a picturesque ten acres overlooking the water.

As she drove up the meandering drive to the faded wooden building that housed both the funeral home and the crematorium, Mazie noticed that the grave sites were well maintained along the drive, but what she assumed to be the older section of the graveyard along the water's edge was badly overgrown. Along the cliff top, the gravestones were ancient, many having fallen over, and others crumbled from neglect.

She parked in front the entrance and then checked her reflection in the rear-view mirror. She realized she looked far too uptight to pass as a grieving widow.

Mazie slipped off the elastic band that held her hair in a tight bun behind her head. Her fair fell loosely around her face and shoulders. She tussled her hair with her fingers, so it looked a bit unkempt. She then pinched her cheeks until her eyes watered.

She took a few deep breaths, slung her purse over her shoulder, and stepped out of the truck.

Mazie walked into the building. A pleasant woman in her early twenties wearing a diamond studded nose ring and a colorful beaded sarong and a gypsy scarf greeted her. The girl sat behind an antique oak desk with a computer screen in front of her, a phone beside her, and a printer at her back.

The office was open and airy, which was a good thing considering the dark oak paneled walls and beige tiled floors. The space was warm and inviting in an old library kind of way.

"May I help you," the woman asked in a voice so soft and innocent that Mazie had to step closer to hear her.

The girl smelled of cinnamon candy and incense.

"I'd like to talk to someone about services for my husband," Mazie mumbled in her best bereaved widow's voice. She pulled out a tissue and blew her nose.

"Oh, I am sorry for your loss," the girl responded, sounding more chipper than consoling.

"Thank you," Mazie sniffed, hoping she wasn't overdoing it.

"I'll page Mr. Deeds for you. He's our Funeral Director and Manager," she offered, hitting a button on her phone.

"Mr. Deeds to the front office," the woman said into the handset.

The loudspeaker blared above their heads, the sound echoing in a room somewhere beyond the front foyer.

A tall slim man with curly black hair, brown eyes, and a thick coal tar colored soul patch on his chin, strode into the office. His movements were graceful, his strides long, his fingers elegant, the nails clipped short and buffed to a sheen.

"Hello, I am Mr. Deeds, both Funeral Director and Manager of Angel's Gate Funeral Home," he introduced himself. "And you are?"

"Mazie...," Mazie stumbled, covering her error with a sniff. "Mrs. Gary Saunders, I should say, but now it's just Mazie Saunders."

"Oh, I am so sorry for your loss," Deeds replied, picking up one of her hands and patting it gently, a practiced look of sympathy on his face.

The firmness of his grip and the hard calluses on his palms surprised Mazie. It was incongruous with the rest of his facade.

"Thank you," Mazie whispered, forcing a sad smile.

"I assume your husband has just passed?"

"Yes, cancer took him much too early."

"That is so sad, but we here at Angel's Gate Funeral Home are here to help you as best we can," Deeds said expertly. "Are you a member of the Memorial Society if I may be so bold?"

"No, my husband thought he'd live forever. I know he would like an old-fashioned burial though with a nice oak coffin. No cremation for him," Mazie stuttered, dabbing at her eyes. "I want to get him a nice big granite stone, one that will last a hundred years."

Deed's face twitched.

Mazie could see he was struggling to keep his gaze somber and not break into a delighted grin.

"Well, let me show you to our casket and stone display room," he offered, holding out his arm for her to take.

Mazie smiled and wrapped her arm under his. Once again, the detective was surprised. Callused hands, powerful muscles, firm grip. She idly wondered what Mr. Deeds did in his spare time. He obviously wasn't a pianist like her first impression implied.

Mr. Deeds escorted the Widow Saunders to a side room. There were *six caskets set on platforms, laid three in a row: an ornate black cherry casket with gold handles and black velvet interior, a red maple casket with brass handles and a rose colored silk interior, three oak caskets of various shades with black, red, and blue velour interiors, and a plain pine casket, the Orphan Annie completing the six-pack. Across from them was a line of gray, brown, black, and red granite gravestones with angels carved on the smooth surfaces.*

Deeds steered her towards the black cherry casket, the most expensive one, Mazie assumed.

"This is our Cadillac line of caskets," Deeds crooned. "We can change the black velvet to another color or change the fabric to silk, cotton or velour, whichever your preference."

"Will cherry last as long as oak," Mazie asked, not wanting to seem to be too much of a push over.

"Definitely. The wood is treated," he purred.

"And I see you have several colors of gravestones to choose from too," she crooned, stepping towards the stones and running a hand down the black one, as if admiring it.

"Yes, we can inscribe it with anything you like," he said amiably.

"I am quite taken with that cherry casket and this black gravestone, but I must say that on the drive in I noticed that some of the cemetery seemed to be in quite a state of disrepair. If I choose to bury my dear Gary here, how do I know that when I am gone his grave will be kept up," she asked innocently.

Deeds' face darkened, but he quickly recovered and smiled down at her.

"If you mean the gravesites along the water … yes, they are a tad unkempt, but you see years of waves and weather crashing against it has undercut the cliff. It is quite dangerous. I can't risk my staff and…well, the bodies there are very old and it's not as if they are going to walk in here to complain. I can assure you we have no zombies here," he said.

Zombies?

Where did that come from?

Mazie's eyebrows shot up.

The Funeral Director of the Angel's Gate Funeral Home stuttered, realizing what he had just said.

"Ummm, sorry, I've been on a Vincent Price marathon lately," he stammered.

"That's fine, Mr. Deeds, I understand. You must work long hours," Mazie said demurely.

"That I do, Mrs. Saunders," he conceded. "Shall we go into my office and we can complete your order and discuss memorial services?"

"Not right now, Mr. Deeds. I quite like Angel's Gate, but I don't live on the island. My husband and I rented a cottage here regularly. It is...was...one of our favorite vacation spots. I haven't decided if I want my husband to rest here or closer to home," the detective lied smoothly.

"I see," Deeds mumbled, his eyes flashing with anger.

Mazie watched as the Funeral Director once again recovered quickly.

"Why don't I give you my card and you can call me anytime," he said, his voice as sweet as buttercups.

"That would be lovely. Thank you, Mr. Deeds," she murmured back.

Mazie thanked the young gypsy woman at the front desk and shook Mr. Deeds hand before heading back to the ferry.

What a strange man, she thought to herself. Just the kind of man who might saw the feet off corpses, she realized. The motive, however, remained a mystery.

***

Mr. Ephraim Deeds, Funeral Director, Manager, and Zombie killer watched the rusted Ford Bronco leave the parking lot of the Angel's Gate Funeral Home.

"Damn tire kickers," he snarled. "That was a waste of my time."

He turned to his secretary and smiled.

"I'll be in the Prep Room in case the lovely Mrs. Saunders changes her mind," he drawled.

"What time is the service for Mr. Johansen again," the sweet *younger woman asked.*

*"Two o'clock, followed by the graveyard service at 4:00 pm sharp,"
he responded pleasantly.*

"What about Mrs. Hansen?"

*"Ah, the poor dear, had no family. She's in the oven now. It's
just you and me for the scattering of her ashes. We can do that
tomorrow."*

"That's so sad," the secretary cried.

*"Yes, but she has you crying for her and that's something isn't it,"
he consoled his secretary.*

*Mr. Deeds patted her hand, much the same as he did the widow
Saunders.*

His secretary sniffed and beamed up at him.

*There was something to be said for a low IQ, the Funeral Director
mused.*

*"Page me if you need me," he said pleasantly and then headed
downstairs to the crematorium and embalming area.*

*"Okay," she squeaked and then blew her nose into a tissue before
switching her attention back to her bookkeeping.*

*Deeds took the stairs two at a time. He jumped down the last two
and strode quickly towards the crematorium.*

*The crematorium was all polished steel and white ceramic tile. It
was a tiny space, compact and utilitarian.*

*Mr. Johanson lay on a metal gurney, his white hair slicked back,
makeup carefully applied to make him look as if he was fit and ready
to climb Mount Everest instead of being laid to rest beneath six feet
of earth in a couple of hours. He wore a black tuxedo, white silk shirt,
and a bright red bowtie.*

*Mr. Deeds checked the timer above the cremation oven and looked
through the oven window to where the flames were a dull simmer
of what they had been. Miss Saunders was almost done, her body
reduced to ash and a few bits of teeth and bone, too stubborn
to incinerate completely. As cantankerous as the old spinster was
rumored to be in life, so she appeared to be in death, thought
Ephraim Deeds.*

The oven switched off on its own, its cycle complete.

"Well, it appears it's just you and me, Mr. Johanson," the Funeral Director said to the corpse on the table.

Mr. Deeds ran a lint brush over the tuxedo, humming the tune to "Hey, Jude" as he did so. He smiled, satisfied with himself.

"Now, don't you be popping up off the table before our time together has finished," he said earnestly. "Your wife and children will be here soon, and we don't want to give them a fright, plus we have to settle you down in that lovely pine beetle coffin that Mrs. Johanson had specially made for you. I must say that you are going out in style, sir. I'd have never thought pine beetle infected wood once lacquered could look so lovely."

***

Detective Mazie Owen stood on the deck of the passenger ferry as it left Jebediah Island, a set of binoculars glued to her face.

The sun was brilliant. It danced off the waves and created sparkling rainbows above the ferry's wake.

The wind lifted her hair.

She tugged her silken mane back into a ponytail, and then returned to scanning the shoreline with a pair of binoculars before the ferry got too far away from the island's rocky shore.

A kaleidoscope of colorful quaint cottages dotted the shoreline, but she paid little heed to them. Her focus was on a crumbling mausoleum atop a disintegrating cliff.

The detective adjusted the binoculars, zeroing in on the cliff wall below the old gravesites that signaled the end of the Angel's Gate cemetery. As Mr. Deeds had told her, it was a hazardous area. The tide had indeed done a lot of damage to the cliff.

She lowered the binoculars.

Even without the aid, she could see where the waves had created a tall funnel inside the rock wall below the cemetery. The force of the high tide and the wind had created a vast blowhole. Saltwater crashed upwards, narrowing into a giant waterspout as it blew upwards, the saltwater cascading over the hardy gravestones that teetered above it.

"That is a brilliant place to dispose of a body," Mazie murmured.

The Dastardly Mr. Deeds: Part Deux

Betty snorted wine out of her nostrils as she laughed aloud. She grabbed a tissue from the bedside table and blew her nose.

"Seriously, Tiffany, I inspired you to write this... this... I don't know what this is," she croaked.

Betty shook her head sadly as she placed the book to one side and climbed out of bed. She needed a pee break, and that seemed as good a place to stop as any.

Outside her bedroom window, the storm raged on. Hail joined the seventy kilometer per hour winds, hitting the building with machine gun precision.

Her lights flickered and then went out.

"Oh, damn," she cursed.

Betty went to the bathroom in the dark and then felt her way along the wall to the kitchen. She searched the drawers until she found a flashlight.

She opened her catch-all cabinet and rifled around in it until she found a couple of pine-scented candles and a box of matches.

Bottle of wine tucked under an arm, candles in one hand, flashlight in the other, Betty wandered back into the bedroom.

She lit the candles and placed them on the nightstand. The light was warm and inviting, the flame casting gentle shadows on the bedroom walls.

Betty poured herself another glass of Merlot and slipped back under the warm covers. The wine was so dark and rich that the light from the candle flames made it look like blood.

She picked up the book and lifted the wine glass, toasting the writer, her friend, Tiffany Hyde-White. She opened the book back up and let the story unfold.

***

Mr. Deeds stood back as Father Peters read a beautiful eulogy, his words so emboldened that it seemed as if Mr. Johanson was a godlike being sent down from Olympus to help humanity. Ephraim had heard many a fake life story read before and seen many a crocodile dear shed for those he witnessed being laid to rest, but the heartfelt words and wrenching tears of the Johanson family caused him to pull a white handkerchief from his pocket and dab at his eyes.

When the service was over, he signaled his man, Landry, to lower the coffin into the ground. With a hum of a winch and the rattle of cables, the coffin descended into its final resting place.

"Ashes to ashes, dust to dust," Father Peters continued, his solemn voice drifting away the wind. "May you find the Almighty Lord himself waiting to greet you at the Pearly Gates. We shall miss you dearly, my friend."

Mrs. Johanson's son and daughter helped her to the gravesite. Never had there been a more regal widow, Deeds thought.

With a trembling hand, Mrs. Johanson tossed a white lily on top of the casket as it descended into the ground. Her daughter and son each tossed in a red rose.

Behind them the sun was dipping towards the horizon in a glorious display of reds and oranges. The white marble and light grey granite grave markers and huge stone angels in the cemetery shimmered in an aurora borealis of color.

It was a beautiful moment.

The family and friends of Mr. Johanson nodded to Mr. Deeds in acknowledgement as they slowly made their way back to their cars.

"I think the angel's themselves have blessed us today," Father Peters said to Mr. Deeds after the mourners had all gone.

"I do believe you're right Father," Deeds returned with a tip of his hat.

Ever the performance specialist, the Funeral Director wore a black topcoat and black top hat at all the graveside services he attended, whether rain or shine.

"He was a good man. I was glad to hear that Mrs. Johanson chose your services and the Angel's Gate Cemetery to bury my dear friend in," the Father replied.

"I am glad you think so highly of us," Deeds crooned.

"I didn't always, Mr. Deeds, but since you have taken over Angel's Gate, I must say that you are at the top of my list of Funeral Directors to recommend to my flock."

Deeds' hand flew to his heart, and he bowed gracefully to the Father.

"Thank you, that means a lot to me and my staff," Deeds murmured.

Father Peters nodded and then made his way out of the cemetery, stopping once to look at the glorious sunset and then back at his friend's grave. He smiled sadly and then walked somberly towards his car.

"You want I should start filling him in," Pierre Landry asked politely.

"No, it's late. You've done a lot today," Ephraim told his assistant. "I'll look after it myself."

"Are you sure, sir? The backhoe's acting up again. I don't mind waiting until the family's all gone to fill him in just in case it gives out on yer," Landry offered.

"If it does, you can cover Mr. Johanson up first thing in the morning," Deeds said, escorting his assistant back to the main building. "It doesn't look like we need to worry about rain tonight."

"Righto I'll be off," Landry replied happily. His wife had a chicken potpie in the oven, and he couldn't wait to dig into it. It had been a long day. He'd weeded about half of the old cemetery along the west side of the property after some woman made a comment about it today.

"Have a nice night, Mr. Landry," the Funeral Director said.

"I will, sir."

Deeds watched Landry waddle off towards his old pickup truck.

His secretary left at about the same time, waving to him as she left the building. He waved back.

Deeds entered the building by the lower concourse. He stepped inside the mud room and took off his coat and top hat, hanging them carefully on a brass wall hook.

The undertaker then went into the janitor's work room and pulled off his shoes. He polished a scuff off one toe with a rag and then tucked them under a wooden work bench. He tugged an orange work coverall over top of his suit and slipped his feet into a pair of gumboots.

The keys to the backhoe hung on the wall on the key rack. He slipped them into his pocket and then walked over to the tool bench.

Deeds looked over the array of saws, garden sheers, and miscellaneous tools that lined the peg board. He slipped a pair of garden sheers into his pocket and pulled a hacksaw off the wall.

He then walked over to an old cedar trunk that squatted in one corner of the work room and pulled a key ring from out of his pocket. He unlocked the trunk.

The trunk contained used sneakers of all sizes from children's sneakers with bright green and pink glow sticks on the side to popular brands of women's and men's athletic footwear, to some truly tattered Adidas.

He picked out a nearly new pair of black and white Nikes.

Hacksaw in one hand, Nikes in the other, he sauntered back to the gravesite.

He paused for a moment to listen to the waves crashing into the blowhole along the cliff's edge and to smell the scent of cedar, fir, and salt on the wind. The sun hadn't quite set.

He sang one of his favorite Beatles tunes: Penny Lane. He thought it an appropriate send off for Mr. Johanson.

Ephraim raised the coffin back up to ground level, the gears on the winch grinding. As the coffin rose to the surface, he admired the light pine wood with the bluish tint from the pine beetle tracks inside the grain. He ran his hand over the smooth surface and sighed. There was nothing prettier than a fine piece of craftsmanship like this, he thought.

Deeds popped open the latches and looked down at Mr. Johanson.

"Well, I am glad you didn't make a ruckus," Deeds whispered to the corpse. "I am sorry for this, but it needs to be done. Angel's Gate Funeral Home is a zombie free zone."

Deeds raised the hacksaw and leaned forward into the coffin. The saw bit through the dead flesh and neck vertebrae. He left the head in place, satisfied that Mr. Johanson would not claw his way out of the coffin and out of the ground, bent on eating his or anyone else's brains and infecting the world with his Zombie virus. For good measure, Deeds also sawed off the dead man's feet.

Deeds casually removed the dead man's sawed-off feet from the shoes and sized the shoes up against his own.

"Those will fit nicely. Thank you, Mr. Johanson," he said to the man inside the coffin.

Deeds slipped the severed feet into the Nike sneakers and placed them back in the coffin.

"It's not everyone who gets their feet back. I usually toss them into the blowhole for good measure, but you have such a lovely family. The Nikes are quite grand, don't you think," he said, admiring the sneakers. "Do promise me I won't regret this, and you won't find a way to chase after me."

Deeds slammed the coffin lid shut, locked the locks, and then lowered the casket back down into the grave as the sun dipped below the horizon and the stars danced overhead.

Somewhere in the distance a night owl hooted.

The lights popped on outside of the office and the other buildings, the timers kicking on at precisely 6 p.m.

Deeds walked towards the backhoe parked at the far end of the gardening sheds. He hoped it would fire up properly. He really didn't like the thought of Mr. Johanson rising from the dead and dragging himself into the prep room in search of a needle and thread to sew his head and feet back on.

***

Betty burst out laughing. She laughed so hard that she

couldn't breathe.

The candle flames wavered as if someone had swept a hand in front of them.

Betty slipped deeper under the covers.

"Tiffany, if that's you," she said into the blackness, "the depths of your depravity are endless."

The wind rattled the windows.

Betty yelped, startled.

The lights blinked on.

She burst out laughing once again.

Exactly what would you call the indomitable Mr. Deeds: zombie exterminator, zombie killer, lunatic?

Betty took a large swig of wine. The merlot warmed her insides, the aftertaste both oaky and sweet.

"An aging cemetery on a cliff top with crumbling cliffs and a blowhole leaving embalmed bodies in the salt chuck and separated feet in sneakers floating away on the tide isn't any crazier than any other explanation we've come up with," she mused. "The fact that no other body parts have turned up is an issue, but maybe Vi was right and Tiffany was actually on to something."

Betty blew out the candles and turned off her bedside lamp, determined now more than ever to return to Seal Island and hire Reggie to take her out for a spin on his boat.

She drifted off to sleep. Mr. Deeds strode through her dreams, his topcoat billowing out behind him, a saw in one hand, and a pair of severed feet in the other.

On Bichons and Psychic Cataclysms

Rainbow sat at the kitchen table in the now refurbished log home, a German shepherd and a Coon Hound laying on the hardwood floor at her feet, their eyes watching her intently as she quietly discussed life with the black and white Bichon dog sitting on the table, its breathing ragged and overbite visible despite the groomer's best attempts to hide it.

"Mitzi, you mustn't let your emotions get the better of you," Rainbow crooned, one hand scratching behind each of the Bichon's ears. "Mummy doesn't love you any less because she's got a new man in her life. This peeing in his shoes and on his side of the bed must stop. You understand that don't you?"

The dog tried to look away, but Rainbow wasn't having any of it. She gently lifted the dog's face up, so she looked directly into Rainbow's blue eyes.

"Look at me, please," she said softly. "Yes, changes are scary, but this acting out doesn't become you. You're much too old for this kind of behavior. I'm going to suggest that Mummy's new beau spend some quality time with you, maybe take you for a ride in his car or motorboat. What do you think of that?"

The little Bichon squirmed in her hands almost knocking Summer River's dog-eared sunflower clad diary and a pile of mail off the table. The German shepherd and Coon Hound whined and thumped their tails loudly at the mention of a car ride.

Rainbow frowned at the little dog, and lifted it up, placing it gently on her lap. She brushed a stray hair out of her face and then shoved the mail into a neat pile and placed the diary on top to hold it down.

A loud knock on the door startled Rainbow.

The hound bayed, the Bishon yipped, and the German shepherd growled as it leapt to its feet.

"Sit," Rainbow commanded, rising from her chair, her Indian print skirt flowing out behind her. "And stay."

The dogs did as commanded.

Another loud knock shattered Rainbow's peaceful communion with the naughty Bichon.

"Hello," she said timidly as she opened the door.

Three old men stood there. One was tall and slim, another was broad-chested with hands as big as a catcher's mitt, while the third was strikingly handsome for his age despite his Rudolph red nose and bloodshot eyes.

They startled Rainbow. She recognized all three of them from Summer's old photos. The photos on the wall were packed inside a box in the barn, still waiting for someone from the Rivers family to come and pick them up.

"Can I help you," she asked politely.

The aura of the slim senior in his early eighties was bright yellow while the barrel-chested man's aura was green, and the other one's aura was a muddy blue shot with red. Her inner alarms went off. The hair on her arms and the back of her neck rose like porcupine quills.

The shepherd, sensing her discomfort, rumbled a warning.

"I know we're a wee bit late," said Archie Bruce, holding out a bottle of white Chablis in offering.

"But better late than never," finished Barney Whyte, holding up two bottles of moonshine.

"And I brought a case of draft for your husband," Stew Mann added.

The grin Stew Mann gave her made her take a step back.

The shepherd stood up and hung his head, his eyes fixed on the doorway and the men who blocked it. He took a few steps closer to Rainbow, despite her command to stay.

A shiver rippled up and down Rainbow's spine.

It would be inhospitable not to offer these three men tea, but still she wavered. There was something not right with the man still holding up the two bottles of moonshine. There was a wicked gleam in his eyes as he looked over her head and examined the kitchen.

Rainbow wished her husband and Blue were at her side, but also knew that Bear and Brew would protect her. Even Mitzi would in a pinch.

The shepherd's rumble turned into a fierce growl.

"It's all right, Bear," Rainbow said to the dog, although she didn't really feel that way. "Please come in. Can I make you a tea?"

"Oh, your husband's not home," Barney asked innocently.

"No," Rainbow answered, trying to keep the tremble out of her voice. She wondered why she felt so threatened by this man in particular. "He'll be back tomorrow. He's gone to pick up some laying hens in Vancouver."

"I'm so glad that you and your husband are going to work the farm," Archie said earnestly, offering her the wine.

"Thank you, but we don't drink," Rainbow said, declining the bottle.

Archie looked dejected.

Rainbow smiled and took the bottle from him anyway.

"Sometimes we have family here and my mother-in-law loves white wine," she said.

Archie beamed at her.

Rainbow placed the bottle of wine on the table beside the mail and Summer's diary.

Archie noticed the diary and his face reddened. He caught Barney's eye and nodded towards it imperceptibly. Barney blanched when he saw the worn and faded diary on top of the table.

The ruddy faced man inched toward it, but the shepherd and the Coon Hound both uttered a warning growl.

Barney backed off, keeping a wary eye on the shepherd. The dog watched his every move. The Coon Hound wagged its tail twice but then stopped. It looked from the shepherd to Rainbow for guidance and settled on a guttural whimper.

"He's not going to bite us, is he," Stew asked, his voice

cracking.

"Oh, no, not unless I tell him to," Rainbow chirped. She smiled down at the dog and patted his head. He glanced up at her, devotion in his eyes. "Poor dear didn't like his job. We're working on finding him a new one."

"And what was his job," Barney queried.

"Bear worked security at the airport. He stopped eating and his handler sent him to me to see what I could do. Bear hated the noise and all the crowds. He's one of the best Cocaine dogs they ever had, they told me, but he'd rather live a quiet life," Rainbow said cheerily.

"Drugs, eh," Barney mused, his eyebrows rising perceptibly.

"Seal Island might not be the best place for him if he doesn't like drugs," Archie joked.

"Ah, Arch, it's only weed we got here," Stew chimed in. "He doesn't mind pot, does he? If'n he does, you better keep him muzzled if you walk him to the pub, especially if Reggie is around."

"I don't think so. It is my understanding that the dogs are trained for specific drugs. Bear was trained to search out cocaine and amphetamines," Rainbow said. "I'll ask Bear about it later though."

The men exchanged a puzzled glance.

"I'm sorry, where's my manners? Tea? I have herb teas and Black tea if you prefer," she asked them.

"Really, we just wanted to introduce ourselves and bring over a housewarming present," Archie said. "I'm Archie Bruce, and these two cads are my mates, Stew Mann, who owns the pub, and Barney Bruce, our illustrious moonshine guru."

Barney bowed and with a flourish handed Rainbow the two bottles of moonshine.

Rainbow laughed and placed the bottles of moonshine beside the bottle of wine on the kitchen table.

"Ahhhh... and I thought your hubby might like a cold one, what with all the work we see you're doing around here," Stew stammered.

Rainbow's apprehension dissipated. Archie Bruce seemed a gentle and honorable man and the pub owner was pleasant too. The moonshine guru though, he was another matter. Bear sensed it too.

"We won't trouble you for long, not with your husband gone. Wouldn't be right," Archie said.

Rainbow smiled warmly at him.

"Is that Mable's Bichon," Stew asked, reaching out to pet the Bichon.

The dog nipped him.

"Yep, definitely Mable's dog," Stew yelped, pulling his hand away.

The men laughed.

"I hear she's taken to doing her business in Barry's slippers," Barney guffawed.

"Simple case of jealousy," Rainbow said. "We're working our way through it today."

"What are you a vet or something," Stew asked.

"No, I'm a pet psychic," Rainbow replied earnestly. "I talk to them and listen to what they have to say. You can tell a lot about what an animal is thinking and feeling by its actions."

"So, the shepherd told you it doesn't like its job, and the Bichon told you it hates Barry," Stew asked, an incredulous look on his face. "What about the hound?"

"Brew is only a pup. He has a high prey drive. I'm working at telling him when it's okay to chase and when it's not. He likes to tree his owner's prize Siamese cats. The cats don't like it very much and being Siamese have launched a campaign to teach him a lesson. He's finding it hard to learn, despite the several stitches in his back where they leapt out of the tree and sunk all their claws into him."

"That must have hurt," Barney muttered.

"Maybe you can come over to my place and talk to Peaches. She's been off her food since that idiot cop tasered her," Archie queried.

"Oh my, you own that poor cow," Rainbow wailed.

"Yeah, she just hasn't been the same," Archie moaned. "She's downright moonie. She hardly eats and even Gertie can't seem to get a rise out of her."

"Arch, that cow's always been moonie," Barney joked.

"How about tomorrow afternoon," Rainbow offered. "It's on the house. Frank and I have been discussing your poor cow, and he told me I should ask who owns it and help out."

Rainbow spontaneously hugged Archie.

Archie grinned at his mates over top of her head.

"You come over any time. I'm sure Peaches will be happy to talk to someone who understands what she's going through."

Archie's two friends guffawed. Archie shot them an evil look.

"Consider it done. I'll be over after lunch," Rainbow agreed.

Barney tried once more to inch toward the table where the diary was, but the Coon Hound launched himself at him, barking furiously.

Rainbow caught the gangly pup in mid-air.

"Brew, that's enough," she said, forcing him into a sit. "I don't know what's got into him."

"I do," Archie mumbled under his breath, casting a warning look towards his buddies.

Barney backed slowly towards the door.

"Right, we'll be off then," Stew chimed in. "Since you don't drink, I'd be happy to share a brew with any of your family when they visit, and the next burger at the pub is on me."

"That's kind of you," Rainbow responded, not having the heart to tell the pub owner that she was a vegan.

"See you tomorrow, Rainbow," Archie said.

Rainbow gasped. *How did he know her name?*

"It's a small island. Everyone knows your name," Archie added, noticing her look of surprise.

"And your secrets," Stew blustered.

Rainbow held Brew by the collar as the men left the cabin. Her smile faded.

"You don't like those men much, do you, buddy," she said to the Coon Hound. He wagged his tail.

The shepherd stood up and nosed her hand.

"Good dog, Bear. I know, you don't like them either. Archie seems okay though."

The shepherd yawned and lay back down.

The Bichon yipped and yipped.

Rainbow turned around to see Summer's ghost standing in the doorway between the kitchen and the living room. Summer pointed at her diary and then pointed towards her bedroom.

The ethereal woman got more agitated as Rainbow stood, routed to the spot.

The German shepherd woofed.

The Coon Hound bayed.

The Bichon peed on the table in response.

"Okay, I get it. Hide the diary. Just let me clean up Mitzi's mess first," Rainbow said, retrieving a washcloth from the sink.

Yellow liquid rolled across the table towards the stack of envelopes. She wiped up the mess and turned towards her ghostly visitor, but Summer had disappeared once again.

Rainbow sighed.

She looked at all the alcohol stacked on the floor and the kitchen table and felt mentally drained. Nothing good would come from having that much booze in the house. Her husband wasn't an alcoholic, but he could get nasty when he drank.

Rainbow was happy that Archie had asked her for assistance with his cow. She liked him. He had a pleasant way about him and was open to her healing abilities. She was sure that the cow was feeling both devastated and betrayed by being hit with a stun gun.

The pub owner was a bit shady, but she had the feeling that he was harmless enough. That Barney Whyte though. She had never seen an aura so muddy. She hoped he didn't visit her again, especially when she was alone.

Maybe she should talk to Frank about keeping Bear. She already loved the dog, and he was attuned to her feelings. Blue was Frank's dog. The Heeler loved her, she knew, but was happiest when he accompanied Frank out to the barn and on his trips to the Lower Mainland to pick up the chickens and pheasants.

She tossed the pee-soaked cloth into the sink and wandered into the living room. The dogs followed at her heels.

She sat down on a yoga mat on the floor, cross-legged amidst the three dogs. The Bichon cuddled up her lap and went to sleep. The shepherd and the hound made themselves comfortable on either side of her, just happy to be touching her.

Rainbow pulled the amethyst crystal she kept on a leather thong around her neck out from under her sweater and cupped it in both hands.

"Ohhhmmmm," she hummed, rocking slowly back and forth, emptying her mind. "Ohhhhmmmm."

She closed her eyes and let her astral spirit float upwards and out of the house, across the strait and to the mainland, drifting to a stop at Horseshoe Bay where her husband played fetch with Blue on the beach while he waited for the ferry to dock. Her husband's and the dog's auras glowed like Roman Candles against the low-slung clouds in the inlet and the rain-soaked streets at their backs.

She smiled, her spirit rejoicing. Rainbow had waited too many years to meet the man who understood her and accepted her for who she was.

Blow Holes

Betty sat on the hard-plastic seat inside the glass-walled passenger area of the Seal Island Ferry reading *The Dastardly Mr. Deeds,* a tight-lipped smile on her face. Today, she was the only passenger.

The seas were choppy, and the sky was grey. The rain had stopped for the moment, but the black clouds on the horizon signaled that more was coming.

The boat heeled to starboard, broadsided by a rogue wave.

Betty flew sideways, the book skipping across the deck. She grabbed a handrail for balance and cautiously retrieved the book.

They were fast approaching the ferry dock.

Betty tucked the book into her backpack and braced herself for a rocky landing. She wasn't disappointed.

It took an extra two crewmen to tie the small passenger ferry up to the swaying dock as the boat bucked on its lines. One of the crew helped her off the pitching boat and onto the slippery dock.

Reggie's trawler was moored kitty-corner to the ferry. Betty thought about knocking on the cabin door, but there were no lights on in any of the windows.

Betty slipped her backpack over her shoulder and walked crab-legged across the dock. It wasn't pretty, but it was effective. She didn't end up in the water screaming for help.

She leapt safely onto the ground and looked back at the moored boats in the marina. There weren't many at this time of year, mostly trawlers and seiners. All of them were bucking against their mooring lines. Three crewmen were battening down the passenger ferry. Obviously, it was too rough to make the trip back over to Vancouver Island. There would be no more adventures at sea for her today.

The pub looked to be doing an active business. She thought of stopping in to see if Reggie was there but decided to check in with her father and possibly head over to Andy's house to snoop through his papers.

She sighed.

Would she ever think of Andy's house as her home?

She wasn't sure. Maybe spending some time there alone would quiet the ghosts.

Betty trudged up North Shore Road, shoulders and head bent into the wind. The wind was bitter, and ice tinged. It stung her cheeks and froze her ears.

She paused in front of the Bone's Bailiwick sign at Vi's house. It was funny how she already thought of Bone's Bailiwick as belonging to Vi instead of Eliza and Wally.

Betty smiled.

The 'For Sale' sign had been removed. She guessed that Vi had decided to keep the cottage after all.

Betty's steps felt lighter as she walked the rest of the way to her father's house.

She unfastened the chain on the metal gate at the end of the lane. Gertrude heard her and raced towards her, the pig's tail wind milling in faster and faster circles.

"Hello, Gertie. Who's a good pig," Betty chattered away to the pot-bellied pig. She rubbed her snout and handed the pig a dog biscuit she pulled from her pocket.

The pig snuffled and squealed with delight, so exuberant that she almost knocked Betty off her feet.

Betty roared with laughter.

A bright fluttering in the branches of the apple tree caught her eye.

She pushed Gertrude aside and looked up.

A dread-locked youthful woman in a hand-woven coat of many colors, bright pink ear mufflers, and a turquoise woolen scarf, balanced on her heels inside the V in the middle of the apple tree's large limbs. The woman gazed into the big brown eyes of the Jersey cow. Peaches' stared right back at the woman, whether from interest or the result of hypnotism, Betty couldn't discern.

Betty hitched the backpack up on her shoulder and strode purposefully towards the house, not sure what to make of the scene. Gertrude followed hot on her heels, apparently quite upset by the goings-on.

The pig followed Betty into the house.

"Dad," Betty yelled as she opened the door.

Gertrude raced by her and disappeared into the living room.

"Angel puss is that you," her father called from the living room.

"Yep," she replied, dropping her backpack on the floor and unzipping her coat. "Sorry I didn't call first."

"Oh, you know you don't have to, Angel," her father said as he entered the kitchen.

"Who's the woman in the tree staring into Peaches' eyes," she asked her father.

"Oh, that's Rainbow McDonald. She's helping Peaches get over the 'Incident'," he answered, helping his daughter with her coat.

"The 'Incident'?"

"You know, Peaches getting tasering by that idiot cop, er... detective."

"Yes, he was an idiot," Betty agreed, a twinkle in her eyes. "Exactly how is she helping Peaches?"

"She's talking to her, reading her mind. Rainbow's a pet psychic. Mable swears by her, told me that Mitzi, her Bichon, hasn't once peed in her boyfriend's shoes or on the bed since Rainbow had a chat with her," Archie replied amiably.

"What is wrong with Peaches that she needs a pet psychic?"

"Well, ever since the Incident, she's been off."

"Peaches has always been a little 'off', Dad. I mean, hey, her best friend is a pig," Betty said, amused. And her owner tried to kill them, Betty refrained from adding.

"Well, you haven't seen her since in a few weeks ago. She

hasn't been eating properly and even Gertie couldn't cheer her up. Reggie tried too. She wouldn't even go down to the pub to have a pint. That just ain't natural," Archie said, his eyes tearing up.

Betty felt bad. She knew how much the pig and cow meant to her father. They were more than pets, they were family.

"I'm sorry, Pop, I didn't know. Well, let's hope that Rainbow can help her."

"Oh, I'm sure she can. She's not even charging me for it, she's so concerned for Peaches," he stated matter-of-factly.

Betty snorted back a laugh and turned her back on her father, gazing out the window to where Rainbow McDonald in her coat of many colors had her hands wrapped around the cow's sublime face and was whispering into its ear.

Betty felt like she was in a Monty Python or Saturday Night Live skit.

She waited until she had regained her composure before turning back to her father.

"Anyway, Pops, I am sorry that I didn't call to say I was coming. I just had to get out of the city," Betty explained.

"Well anytime you need to come home, you know you are welcome, isn't she Gertie," he asked the pig.

The pig grunted and snuffled Betty's coat pocket which was now hanging on a peg beside the door.

"Oh, you pig. You should have been born a blood hound," Betty teased Gertrude.

Betty pulled the last Milk Bone from her pocket and gave it to the pig.

"We'll ask Rainbow about that," her father replied.

Betty coughed into her hand, her eyes watering with mirth.

"Hey, did you notice that Vi took the 'For Sale' sign down at the cottage," Betty mentioned.

"Yeah. Barney told me he and Cam made an offer to buy it, but Vi wouldn't sell it to them. Next thing you know, the sign was down. Barney said Camille had quite the tantrum over it."

"Why on earth would Barney and Camille want to buy Vi's

cottage when they already have a stunning oceanfront home?" Betty said, puzzled.

"He got all sauced up at the pub and told Stew and me that she wanted to turn it into a murder themed bed-and-breakfast," Archie grinned.

"Oh, I expect that went over really well with Vi," Betty guffawed.

"I don't think Vi knew. I called her after he told me he tried to buy it and she told me she just couldn't part with the place. I told her how glad I was and that I hoped she'd pop over for tea when she comes back to the island. I'd like to introduce her to Rainbow. I know she'd like that young lady. Don't let the hippy skirts and weird hair fool you. She's one smart girl," Archie added. "She's got a real pleasant way about her."

"Don't you go getting all sweet on her," Betty joked.

"Oh, don't you worry about that," Archie answered earnestly. "My heart is still with your mother and our dear, Eliza, God rest their souls. No more ladies for me, Angel."

Betty strode across the kitchen, pushed the giant pig out of her way, and hugged her father.

"Hah, what's that for," he asked, surprised.

"Do you know how much I love you, Dad," she asked him.

"I do, Angel puss, I do," he croaked.

Betty and her father exchanged sheepish grins. Gertrude head butted her.

"And I love you too, Gertie," Betty laughed.

Archie blushed and then busied himself with putting the kettle on for tea.

"So, did you identify that poor woman that Reg and Stew found washed up on the beach," he asked as he pulled out a box of English Breakfast tea.

"Yeah, it's a sad story. Coroner has already ruled it accidental. The couple had too much to drink. It ended in a fight. Husband passed out. Wife fell and hit her head, rolled off the boat and into the salt chuck. End of story," Betty confided, leaving out the part about Roy the Clown and his unicorn loving gambling addicted young bride. It wasn't a story that her father needed to hear.

"I need to talk to Reggie. Do you have his cell number anywhere, Dad," Betty asked, picking up her backpack and heading for her bedroom.

"You don't have to call. He and the boys are coming over for a round of poker tonight."

"Cool."

"What do you need to talk to him about," Archie asked as he filled the tea pot with hot water.

Gertrude nosed him, looking for more treats.

"That's enough, Gert," he growled.

"Oh, just looking for some advice."

"You aren't gonna start a grow op are you? I don't think Reggie would be happy with the competition, especially now that he's all legal."

Betty laughed.

"No, something else," she said, bolting out of the kitchen before her father asked her any more questions. She didn't know why; she just didn't feel like talking about it right now.

Betty reached the safety of her bedroom and threw the backpack on the chair beside the bed. She pulled out Tiffany's book and made herself comfortable on the bed. She was just getting to the part where Mazie Owen had commandeered a police boat and was heading back to Jebediah Island.

There was a splash of movement outside as Rainbow and the cow galloped side-by-side past her bedroom window, cavorting in the garden like two sprites, one weighing in at nine hundred pounds, the other at one-twenty.

Betty chuckled.

She loved Seal Island.

The McDonalds would fit right in.

She opened the book to where she had bent the corner over on the top of one page and began to read.

***

The Dastardly Mr. Deeds, Chapter Fourteen

Detective Mazie Owen stood beside the captain on the bridge of the police hovercraft as they crested the tops of the waves like greased snowboards on ice, racing towards Jebediah Island.

Her uniform was crisp and fresh, the creases in her hat and pants as sharp as razor edges. Her face was grim: her blue eyes hard, her jaw line tight. The tension in her body caused the veins in her throat and at her temple to throb.

"There," she said, pointing to the north-west side of the island where a volcanic spray erupted into the air high above the blowhole that marked the midway point of the Angel's Gate Funeral Home's cemetery.

The captain told his navigator to adjust his course.

The hovercraft skipped over the Strait.

The boat angled in as close to the shoreline and the blowhole as they could.

Betty was joined by the captain and two of her team members on deck.

Betty and the men with her braced themselves against the roll of the waves as they raised binoculars to their eyes.

"Is that a coffin edge I see hanging out under that white zebra streaked boulder there," the captain asked.

The rotting edge of an old wooden coffin jutted out of the rocky cliff at a forty-five-degree angle, a gaping hole in its side where the handle had once been.

"Sure, looks like it," one of Mazie's partners said.

Mazie zoomed in on the coffin's edge. She then swept the binoculars downwards towards the base of the cliff. Her knuckles whitened as she clamped down on the binoculars.

"Look down below it. That looks like a broken headstone to me. It's just above the high tide line," she growled.

"Good Lord," the captain gasped.

"That's enough to get us a warrant," her partner said. "You sure called it Mazie."

"You really think this is where those severed feet are coming from," the captain queried.

"I'd bet a year's salary that at least some of them are," the detective responded carefully.

"But that wouldn't account for the fact that the feet were all in sneakers. Those gravesites look old. I don't think they had Keds or Adidas when those folks were laid to rest," the captain added.

"No, it wouldn't, but those gravestone markers and that coffin up there will allow us to get a warrant and a team in there. I want to ask Mr. Deeds some pointed questions," Mazie responded. "He's a strange man. I'm hoping a warrant backed up by a squadron of police officers will shake him up."

"Aren't all Funeral Director's a little weird. I mean what kid grows up saying I want to deal with dead people all day," her partner muttered.

"True, but this guy is way past a little weird. You should have heard him talking about there being no zombies in his graveyard," Mazie countered.

"Zombies? Seriously," the captain blurted out.

"What? Does he think the people he buries dig themselves out of their graves at night or something," her youngest partner asked.

The three men and Mazie exchanged startled looks.

"You don't think...," the captain started.

"That he's cutting the feet off of dead people and throwing them in the salt chuck so they can't come after him," one of her partners gasped.

"Like I said, the guy's strange," Mazie said, her voice cracking.

"How on earth do you get a warrant for that," the captain queried.

"You don't. You get a blanket warrant to investigate the blowhole, cemetery, and the Angel's Gate Funeral Home. We seize every saw on the premises and see if they match up to the saw marks on the ankle bones. After that, we pray," she confided.

***

Betty closed the book, her brow furrowed in thought.

She doubted that a zombie crazed undertaker was sawing off feet and throwing them into the salt chuck in real life, but there were lots of old cemeteries on the islands around here. The possibility that some of them were crumbling into the sea wasn't that farfetched.

"What did you know, Tiffany," Betty mumbled to the spider who was building a web in one corner of her ceiling, the heat from the furnace vents making it a harder task than normal task.

"And did what you knew lead to your death?"

Betty turned over and closed her eyes.

She definitely wanted to take a trip around the Gulf Islands and the Coast with Reggie Phoenix to see if there were any blowholes that needed investigating. Exhaustion quickly overtook her, and that was fine with Betty. She hadn't slept properly in months.

The Poker Chip Blues

Archie and his poker crew sat around the kitchen table, glasses of moonshine in front of everyone except the grizzled old fisherman, Reggie Phoenix. Reggie refused to touch the stuff.

Cigar smoke filled the air.

An empty pizza box sat on the counter beside a couple of half-empty bottles of moonshine and a case of beer.

"That hippie chic still outside talking to your cow," Barney asked amused.

"Yep. Peaches seems to enjoy her company," Archie confirmed.

Stew guarded his cards from prying eyes, sure that Barney, sitting across the table from him, had Superman powers and could read his hand.

Archie was more cavalier about it, but then he had his wife to back him up. Her ashes were sitting in a decorative clay urn at the centre of the table.

Reggie was puzzled. He stared at his cards as if the aces, hearts, diamonds, and clubs, were some ancient hieroglyphs of which he had no knowledge.

Barney shrewdly studied everyone's faces before throwing five bucks into the centre of the table.

"I call," Barney challenged the men.

"Oh, damn you," Stew growled, folding his hand.

"You're on a roll tonight, Barney," Reggie mumbled, throwing in his cards.

"What's that, pet," Archie asked, cupping a hand behind his ear, his eyes on the urn. "You think he's bluffing? I think you're right. I'll match your fiver and raise you another."

Archie tossed ten bucks into the pile of bills on the table.

Barney laughed with glee and placed his cards on the table one at a time.

"I got a pair of eights," he said, picking up his glass of home brew. He downed it in one swallow.

"Hah, Mary was right again," Archie said cheerily. "Pair of tens takes it."

"Oh, you cocky so and so," Barney hissed.

"Playing poker with the two of you is a losing cause," Stew grumbled.

"Yah, I don't remember the last time I won a hand," Reggie agreed.

"That's because you're an honest man," Betty chirped as she entered the room. "Mercy, open a window, Pops, it stinks in here."

"That's man smell, honey," Barney winked at her.

"Hey, I'm an honest man too," Stew stated, affronted.

"And the Devil wears high heels," Barney joked.

"Oye," Reggie gasped. "You better make sure he's not listening. That there's dangerous talk, Barney."

Betty laughed.

"Don't worry, Reg, my wife'll clean his clock if he shows up," Archie said with a laugh.

"I wouldn't doubt that for a minute," Barney agreed.

"What's up, Angel," Archie asked.

"I just wanted to ask Reg something," she replied.

"You aren't going to ask him out, are ya," Stew queried.

"By God, we'd never hear the end of it," Barney said.

"Why don't ya let the lady ask her question," Reggie grumbled.

"It's official police business. I need your expertise, Reg," Betty said, ignoring the cheeky grins on the faces of her father and the other men at the table. "I need to hire you and your boat if the weather isn't too bad tomorrow."

"Well, I'd be right pleased to do that, Bet," Reggie agreed, perking up.

Barney slapped Reggie on the back.

Stew glowered.

Archie frowned.

"What's this all about, Angel, seriously. Should I be worried?" Archie asked.

"I just want Reg to help me with one of my cases."

"Which one," Stew countered. "That pretty gal that Reg and I found or Gertie's severed foot?"

"Actually, I found her, Stew. You just came along and drank my beer," Reggie corrected him.

"Oh, Angel solved the case of the Painted Lady," Archie announced proudly.

"What painted lady," Reggie asked, puzzled. "That poor girl wasn't painted. Didn't have no make-up on either from what I remember."

"We called her the Painted Lady because of the fancy unicorns and rainbows painted on her fingernails," Betty told Reggie. "Turns out it was an accidental drowning, not murder."

"That's good. Not that the young girl drowning wasn't bad, I'm just saying that I'm glad it wasn't the Seal Island Curse," Stew stuttered.

"The Seal Island Curse," Betty asked, as confused as Reggie looked.

"You know, all those strange deaths. First, Eliza, then, Summer River, and lastly, our lovely Tiffany," Stew said, making the sign of the cross on his chest. "I still miss that girl."

"We all do," Archie agreed sadly.

"I'm just saying that I think Seal Island is cursed. Old lady Mickelson up and dropped dead two weeks ago too. What do you have to say about that?"

"Old lady Mickelson was ninety-seven, Stew," Barney said.

"I don't really like the idea of you going out with Reggie alone," Archie added.

"What makes you say that?" Reggie wailed, standing up. "You think I'd ever harm, Betty. You've done gone senile, you have."

"That's not what I meant," Archie said, back-peddling.

"I need Reg to take me out to look at some of the islands, maybe get a handle on where that foot came from," Betty assuaged her father. "Reg knows these islands and the tides better than anyone."

"That I do, Bet, that I do," Reggie agreed, taking his seat at the table once again. "Come by the boat around nine tomorrow. I'll have her fueled up and ready to go."

"Thanks, Reg," Betty said, patting him on the shoulder.

Reggie blushed.

Betty walked over to the coat rack and slipped a red and black checkered lumberjack shirt over top of her sweater.

"Where you off to now," her father asked.

"Check my house out," she said, waving a hand towards the road.

"You're coming back right," Archie asked.

"Dunno. I might sleep there," Betty mumbled. "I'm not sure. I can't stand all the male pheromones in here."

Three of the men chuckled; Betty's father did not.

Betty left the men to their poker chip blues and headed out the door.

Gertrude was waiting for her.

Gertrude raced towards her, pig tail whipping around and around like an out-of-control merry-go-round. She snuffled Betty's hand looking for treats.

Betty grinned and ruffled her snout.

She wandered over to Rainbow, planning on introducing herself, Gertrude at her side.

Rainbow was once again sitting in the tree staring at the Jersey cow.

Betty wasn't sure if she should interrupt the woman or not. Gertrude didn't mind and squealed loudly.

***

Out of her peripheral vision, Rainbow noticed Betty and the pig standing there.

The pig's 'hello, here I am' squeal was loud and clear.

Rainbow chuckled and dropped to the ground.

Peaches bawled a greeting to her friend.

"Sorry," Betty apologized, "But Gertie's manners are sadly lacking sometimes."

"That's okay, I quite adore her," Rainbow said, her eyes sparkling. She kissed the cow on the nose and then wrapped her graceful arms around Gertrude's neck and hugged her.

"I'm Betty, Archie's daughter," Betty said, stepping forward, and extending her hand.

"Rainbow McDonald," Rainbow acknowledged, shaking Betty's hand. "I've heard a lot about you."

"Oh, dear, all bad, I expect. Which of the men inside blabbed my secrets," Betty joked good-naturedly.

"None. Your father adores you."

"I adore him too," Betty beamed. "And he sure loves that cow and our silly pig. How is Peaches doing? Dad told me she's off her food. Not a good sign with either of these two."

"I think she's doing better. We've had a good chat and a play around the garden. That really lifted her spirits. It seems it wasn't the tasering per se that got her going, it was a delayed reaction to all the changes in her life," Rainbow casually remarked.

"How so," Betty asked, intrigued.

Rainbow was pleased. She had expected opposition. The moonshine guru and the pub owner's comments about Betty had led her to believe that Betty was a no-nonsense, closed-minded person, jaded by the world, and hardened by loss.

Rainbow also had an aversion to police officers having spent much of her earlier years living on the street. She couldn't read Betty's aura, which was unusual, but given the detective's job, Rainbow expected Betty had developed the ability to shield herself from psychic manipulation and viewing.

The sad eyed and world-wary woman standing before her appeared open and frank. Rainbow took an instant liking to her.

"Peaches moons for the other, the one that's gone."

"You mean Andy," Betty gasped.

"Yes. He was her world, except for Gertrude. She spent a lot of time with him. He was all she knew. Living here makes her feel like she's on an extended vacation. It's not home. Do you understand what I mean?"

Betty looked thoughtful for a moment.

As Rainbow waited for her to answer, Summer's ghost appeared behind Betty.

The cow and pig stepped backwards, alarmed. The cow mooed, and the pig grunted a warning.

"Shhhhh," Rainbow hushed them.

"She won't hurt you," she whispered into the animals' ears, glancing sideways at the apparition.

Betty shivered and looked to her right, sensing the ghost, but unable to see it.

Summer smiled at Betty and then turned towards Rainbow. She pointed at Betty, herself, and then motioned with her hands like she was opening the pages of a book and writing in it.

"The diary," Rainbow asked the ghost. "You want me to give Betty the diary?"

The ghost nodded and disappeared like fog in the sunshine.

"What," Betty queried, puzzled.

Betty looked to her right and then her left. She appeared to shake herself out of a trance.

"I found something in our house I think you should see."

"Oh, what is that?" Betty asked, mildly shaken.

"Summer's diary. I think Summer wants you to have it."

"Summer kept a diary, did she," Betty said, her eyes narrowing. "Have you read it?"

"I've read some of it, but only the part where she talks about building the log house. The rest I felt was too personal and I wasn't comfortable reading it."

"Indeed."

Now the policewoman was coming out, Rainbow thought.

"Perhaps you could come tomorrow and pick it up," Rainbow asked.

She saw Betty relax.

"I will, but it won't be until late. I've an errand to do first and

I don't know how long it will take. Thank you though. There are some things about Summer's death that still bother me. Perhaps her diary can shed some light on them."

Betty turned to leave.

"I'm about to head home now myself," Rainbow blurted. "Are you heading across the road to Peaches' old home?"

"Yes. It's my home now," Betty shrugged, looking uncomfortable.

Betty paused as if waiting for Rainbow to respond.

Rainbow didn't know what to say so remained silent.

"Oh, I see what you're getting at. You think I should take Peaches with me," Betty ventured.

"Yes, she would like that," Rainbow smiled. "I think it would help her with her abandonment issues."

Rainbow lifted her shoulder bag off of a branch in the apple tree. She had to hang it high, away from the pig's prying nose.

"Can't hurt," Betty said, softening.

Rainbow and Betty wandered down the lane. The pig and the cow fell into step beside them.

"It was nice to meet you, Rainbow," Betty said opening the gate to let everyone out.

"Ditto," Rainbow said. "Stop by for tea anytime you would like too. It's lonely out there sometimes and I wouldn't mind the company."

"I'll do that," Betty agreed.

With a quick kiss on the pig and cow's noses, Rainbow danced down the road.

Rainbow felt good. It was a productive day. She had helped a homesick cow and made a new friend.

She laughed, swirling her skirts around her as she broke into a jog.

Frank would be home soon too.

Rainbow leapt into the air and high-fived a low hanging cedar bough, a colorful sprite in a darkening world filled with secrets and betrayal.

Home Sweet Home

Betty watched the youthful woman parade down the road in a rainbow of fabric: yellow, orange, fuchsia, emerald green, purple and sky-blue layers of wool and cotton swirled around her as she walked, jogged, and skipped merrily along.

Despite her oddities, Betty liked Rainbow McDonald.

Betty chuckled as she walked up the meandering driveway to what she still thought of as Andy's house, the Jersey cow and pot-bellied pig following her as if she were the Pied Piper.

But it's my house now, she silently corrected herself.

Betty stopped and looked up at the rambling gables of the Victorian era style house. For a minute, she thought she saw Andy standing in his bedroom window, a twisted grin on this face, his hands beckoning her to come in.

"I'm tired, Gertie," she mumbled to the pig.

The pig squealed and nosed her hand.

Betty rubbed the pig's stubbly head and exhaled the breath she hadn't realized she had been holding.

"What do you think, my friends," she asked, stumbling upon her words.

Peaches bawled and trotted off towards the barn. Gertrude waited, as if unsure if she should leave Betty alone.

Betty burst out laughing.

"Go on, off you go," she ordered the pig.

Gertrude raced off to join Peaches.

"Guess I better order some hay," she said to the wind.

Betty drew a large key ring out of her pocket. She unlocked the front door and stepped inside the foyer.

Silence greeted her.

She shrugged off her coat and gumboots and made her way into the kitchen. A smattering of fingerprint dust covered the kitchen counters, sink and cupboards.

The snow topped Watchtower Mountain was visible through the patio doors and kitchen window. The snow line was low, almost reaching the valley, but not quite. A herd of deer grazed in the meadow.

With a start Betty realized that if she sold her condo and took early retirement, which she could since she was now fifty-four and had thirty-two years on the force, this could be her view every day for the rest of her life.

She placed a hand over her breast. The pain in her heart was unbearable. Her throat constricted, not with fear or loathing, but awe at the thought of how much Andy must have loved her to have changed his Will to leave this house to her. She wished fervently that she had told him how much she had truly loved him back.

Betty felt dizzy.

She sat down heavily on a kitchen chair.

Tears streamed down her face.

She brushed them away and absently stared at the rain-soaked fields and forests.

Peaches and Gertrude chose that moment to gallop around the side of the house and into the meadow, startling the deer. The deer bounded off into the forest.

Betty laughed; the spell broken.

"Home sweet home," she murmured.

She stood up and opened the sink cupboards. She pulled out some earth-friendly lime scented cleaning spray, a rag, and began cleaning up the mess the forensic team had left.

Before long, the kitchen sparkled once again.

She made herself a cup of mint tea and wandered upstairs, tea in hand.

She crept into Andy's room.

His shirts, slacks, and suit jackets still hung in the closet. A suitcase was open on a suitcase rack inside the large walk-in closet. The corners on the bed were regimental straight.

Her hands trembled.

Betty inhaled sharply and steeled herself for the job ahead. She brushed away a tear and went to work packing up the clothes in the closet for delivery to the local thrift shop, all except the two tweed jackets with the leather patches on the arms that were Andy's favorites. She loved those jackets and couldn't bear to part with them.

Betty stripped the bed and took the sheets and comforter downstairs to the laundry room.

She sniffed the bed sheets, Andy's musky smell and that of Irish Spring soap permeated the cotton.

She brushed away more tears.

Betty deposited the sheets and comforter on top of the washer and walked away, not having the heart to wash them. She made her way back upstairs.

She found a homemade quilt and a set of lacy white sheets inside the hall cupboard. Betty realized that they must be Marilyn's, Andy's mother. A smile tugged at her lips as she lifted them up and took them to the bedroom.

Betty had liked Marilyn. She was quite the character, her language bold and her life colorful, a stark contrast to her son who liked the world to be black and white. It was strange how different the two were.

Betty didn't like the changes that Andy had inflicted upon the house. She missed the vibrant terracotta walls in the kitchen and the sage green and beach colored walls and furniture in the living room.

The feeling of not belonging suddenly dissipated.

The house was hers now. She could revive the old girl and bring back its former warmth and charm.

The memory of her mother and Marilyn, two peas-in-a-pod, sitting on the over-stuffed couch in the living room, drinking tea, and chatting about canning, composting, and men, in that order, made her laugh.

She knew why Andy left her the house.

Love, yes, but something much stronger than that.

She had wonderful memories here. She could have sworn that Marilyn was standing over her shoulder, smiling.

She could hear the Nobel Laureate now – 'do what you want, dear. Change it back. Make it a happy house.'

Betty grinned as she made the bed, relishing the look and feel of the red, white and blue triangle quilt atop of it. She stretched out on the bed and looked out the window at the rows of Western Red cedar and fir trees that lined the driveway.

The house creaked, as if sighing with relief.

Betty was home.

Her father would be heartbroken when she went to pick up her things, but in the end, like every father, he wanted what was best for his daughter.

Maybe when she got back to the city, she'd even talk to a Realtor about selling her condo.

Betty rolled over.

Andy lay in the bed beside her, his head on the pillow, one hand tucked beneath it. A wave of unruly hair fell over one eye. He pushed the hair from his face. His eyes were alight with mischief and desire.

Betty's breath caught in her throat. She reached for him, but her fingers found only empty air.

Andrew McDowell, writer, lover, and madman wouldn't be back, but his story would not end in this way. There were too many questions left unanswered.

"I swear that I'll find out what happened to you," she whispered into his pillow. "I won't stop until I have answers."

Who had slipped Andy the drugs that turned him from a lovable Golden retriever into a raging madman in record time? The change was too dramatic and too fast.

She hoped Summer's diary would shed some light on the mysteries that haunted her dreams.

With renewed resolve, Betty leapt out of bed and strode down the stairs, intent on retrieving her belongings from her father's house. The lethargy that had dogged her since Andy's death sloughed off her. It was time to make some changes, and this was just the start.

Angel's Heavenly Gate

Betty stood beside Reggie Phoenix on the cramped bridge of his seiner. The cleanliness of the boat had surprised her. Either Reggie was a neat freak which didn't seem likely, or he had been up all-night cleaning the bridge and deck just for her. The thought of Reggie, on his knees with a scrub brush in hand, a bottle of lemon pledge and a dust rag, made her smile.

The Persephone was a 1940 wooden seiner built in Vancouver when the shipyards there were in their heyday. The hull was painted black and the trim was fire engine red. Twin masts that once held a giant spool were also black. Instead of the net rigging, there was a dozen crab traps tied down on the worn wooden planks of the deck.

While the ship would have been a prized possession in any maritime museum, the bridge was modern and up to date with fish finders, GPS, several types of satellite navigation, and a satellite radio. The only original items were the old wooden wheel, oak trim, and a brass ship's bell.

The bridge smelled like coffee and lemon oil with a hint of cannabis.

"So, what are ya thinkin'," Reggie asked as he pulled out of the Seal Island harbor, passing by the Seal Island ferry as he did so.

"Well, the Coast Guard seemed to think this foot in particular could have come from northeast of here, somewhere around Texada Island or upwards towards Powell River, but I have a theory," Betty remarked, letting the sentence remain unfinished as she watched the ferry go by. She thought she saw Vi Bone's tiny figure curled up in a blanket amidst the other passengers, but from this distance, she couldn't be sure.

She took a sip of her coffee and thought about how to proceed. Reggie Phoenix was the one person who she believed wouldn't think she was daft if she told him truthfully what was on her mind.

Reggie maneuvered the seiner between the red and green buoys marking the channel into the harbor. The water was calm, but in the distance the strait was choppy, the water a deep slate grey, the winds blistering cold, blowing in from the northeast.

For a moment Betty forgot where she was and what she was saying, the raw power and majesty of the old wooden boat and the rumble of the engine transporting her into another time.

"Ya all right there, Bet," Reggie asked.

Betty glanced his way. Eyes the same color as the water regarded her warmly. His beard, clipped short, was as grey as his eyes. A ruff of equally curly slate colored hair poked out from beneath a Vancouver Canucks toque. The hands that gripped the wheel were strong and scarred. The index finger on the right hand was missing the top half.

With a start, Betty realized that Reggie Phoenix had trimmed his beard and his hair since last night. He wore a clean ivory cardigan and weathered, but clean, blue jeans and comfortable looking hiking boots with solid rubber soles. She didn't know whether to be amused or concerned.

"Sorry, Reggie, I was just admiring the view," she replied.

Reggie blushed, his cheeks turning a deep shade of crimson.

"The strait is quite beautiful with the grey water, white caps, and the grey clouds above it," she told him. "And your boat is a real beauty, Reg."

"Uhhhh... ummm, yes, it is," he stammered. "Thank you, I guess. I love my girl."

"Your girl," Betty queried, confused.

"The *Persephone*."

"Ah, yes, the *Persephone*," she repeated.

Reggie shot her an odd look.

Betty sighed.

"What I tell you can't go any further than the two of us," Betty continued, trying to put the besotted man at ease.

"Of course not, Bet," Reggie said, mildly affronted. "That goes without saying. I like your Da and all, but he and Barney and Stew, they're like old women sometimes, don't ever stop blatherin' on and on and on."

Betty burst out laughing.

"They are at that."

Betty switched her attention to the sea before them. Seagulls floated in the air off to starboard, matching the *Persephone's* speed.

"Vi, Judge Bone, turned me on to one of Tiffany's books. I know this sounds strange, crazy even, but I think Tiff may have been on to something in her rather interesting take on where the severed feet came from," Betty explained. "She has this idea..."

"That the feet were sawed off'a bodies and dropped down the Glory Hole by a zombie killing undertaker," Reggie finished somberly.

"You've read Tiff's books," Betty gasped, surprised.

"Course I have," he grimaced. "I got to say, Bets, but I don't think ya know me very well, even though we've known each other fer years."

Betty protested, but Reggie held up a hand, stopping her short.

"Me and Tiffy were darn good friends. She talked to me about all sorts of stuff. She had me take her out on excursions around the islands, even helped me out with some of my farmin', if you don't mind me sayin' off the record like."

"Off the record, all the way," Betty agreed.

"She was real interested in learning stuff, all sorts of stuff, from farmin' to growin', fishin' to crabbin', how to read the weather and the stars in the sky, and she liked to bounce ideas for some of her books off me too."

Reggie took a sip of his coffee, and turned the wheel, piloting the boat past Bone's Bailiwick and her father's house, perched high on the cliffs of Seal Island.

Betty had the feeling that he was purposefully not looking at her.

"All those men takin' advantage of her didn't sit well with me," he said sadly. "It ain't right what they did. They done used her up and tossed her aside like she was some trollop. Tiffy wasn't no trollop. She was just dyin' to be loved, is all. Hell, ain't we all? It wasn't fair that she should die right when she was finally turnin' her life around."

"On that we both agree, Mister Phoenix," Betty consoled him.

"Now don't ya be callin' me Mister, ya hear," he growled, glaring at her forcefully.

Betty grinned.

"Just tryin' to lighten up the moment, Reg," she said softly. "And by the way, I know exactly what kind of man you are. You're a decent man, Reggie Phoenix, a good man with a big heart. Men like you are hard to find on Seal Island and anywhere else in this big bad world."

Reggie rolled his eyes at her and turned east around the tip of Seal Island.

"It's only a big bad world if'n you let it beat you down. I don't let it, is all."

Betty put a hand on Reggie's shoulder and squeezed it. He was right. She shouldn't paint him with the same brush as she had painted every man in her life, including Andy and sometimes even her father.

Betty sighed as the waves gently crashed against the wooden hull. The boat heaved too as it headed into the wind, the wooden hull groaning as it sliced through the waves.

"I think the question that I should be asking is where are you taking me," Betty queried, looking out the rear window of the cabin as the *Persephone* left Seal Island behind.

"Well, I was thinkin' last night that if you wanted me to take ya out on 'official' business and that if'n that 'official' business was tryin' to figure out where that severed foot that Gertie found came from, and since we've been talkin' about Tiffy, and you been talkin' to Judge Bone about the zombie killing undertaker, that I should take ya to the place that I took Tiffy," Reggie stated matter-of-factly.

"And that is?"

"Why to the Glory Hole of course," he replied.

Betty shouldn't have been surprised.

"And is this Glory Hole on an island with an old cemetery above it?"

"Not quite. The Angel's Heavenly Gate Cemetery is just outside of Lund, on the mainland, to be exact," Reggie said.

Betty's mouth fell open. She closed it with a click of her teeth.

Reggie chuckled.

"Mister Phoenix, have you been holding out on me," Betty stuttered.

"Miss Bruce, I've had far too many concussions in my life to think that far ahead," he confessed.

"Then you are correct, Mister Phoenix, I have underestimated you and I am truly sorry for that," she apologized.

"Well, then let's go visit us a Glory Hole," the old fisherman winked at her, "and stop calling me Mister Phoenix."

Betty and Reggie clinked mugs.

A smug smile crept over Reggie's lips. Betty didn't know whether she wanted to wipe it off his face or kiss him. He had disarmed her, and that didn't happen very often.

***

An hour and a half later, Reggie eased back on the throttle. The *Persephone's* engines slowed to a dull roar.

The sun broke through the clouds. The water glittered with rainbow flashes of silver as small salmon fry and schools of herring leapt above the waves. Seals bobbed in the water like interconnected rafts, flippers up as they gorged themselves on the fry.

Betty let out a long breath at the view of the steep shale cliff inside a narrow inlet just south of Lund, a tiny little village north of the City of Powell River. Atop the cliff stood a weathered church and cemetery looking very much the same as what

Tiffany had written about.

The church was picture perfect, pretty with its weathered siding, leaning fence, and moss-covered granite gravestones. Below the heritage cemetery, a hollowed-out chute in the granite created a blowhole where, during high winds and tides, the water shot geysers of salt water upwards like Old Faithful in Yellowstone National Park.

"The Glory Hole," Betty mumbled under her breath.

"Yep, the Glory Hole," Reggie agreed.

Reggie slowed the boat to trolling speed, keeping it safely away from the dead head logs and unseen boulders beneath the waves.

"Angel's Heavenly Gate was named after Angel Whitaker, the long-lost daughter of the Whitaker family's great-grandfather who was the first pastor here," Reggie informed her. "Rumor had it that he was a hard God-fearin' type with fire and brimstone runnin' through his veins if ya know what I mean. Some say that Angel ran away an eloped with a freighter captain, but others say that Pastor Whittaker got carried away with his preachin' and wound up takin' his daughter's life. To cover up his crime, it is said that he throwed Angel's body into the ocean. God was so angry at the pastor that in his fury, he created the storm of the century and when the waters receded, there was the Glory Hole. They said that the pastor found Angel's body resting against a headstone inside the cemetery, looking like she was laughin' at him. Legend says that Pastor Whittaker went mad and jumped off that there cliff with his daughter's body in his arms, only this time neither the pastor nor his daughter ever came back up."

"Is all that true," Betty asked, with a glimmer of understanding as to where Tiffany came up with the story behind *The Dastardly Mr. Deeds*.

"Who knows which parts are true and which ain't," Reggie replied. "That's the thing about legends, figuring out what's real and what's not takes a powerful lot of spelunking into history."

"Is the church and cemetery still open?"

"From what I hear it is."

"You want me to take us into Lund? I can tie up there if you want and you can go see fer yourself if'n you want," Reggie offered.

"No, I'd like to come back when I'm more prepared," Betty answered.

"All under cover and the like," the old fisherman nodded sagely.

Betty grinned.

"Definitely under cover," she agreed, feeling like Detective Mazie Owen herself.

"But since we're here, why don't we tie up and go for lunch at the dock. My treat," Betty offered.

"They have some of the best fish n'chips around," Reggie said, flashing a hundred-watt smile.

"Super. It's a date then," Betty added, turning to look at the gravestones leaning over the cliffs. They looked just as Tiffany described in her book.

Reggie beamed with pride and fired up the enormous diesel engine.

Stewed, Baked & Fricasseed

A deckhand helped Vi off the ferry just as Archie pulled his battered Dodge up in front of the docks.

Vi wasn't sure how she felt about him yet. His betrayal still stung. His fling with Tiffany Hyde-White was repulsive; there was no excuse for it, not even the proverbial, boys will be boys. Vi barely knew Archie at the time, but it bothered her he had taken advantage of the girl's addictions, no matter how willing a partner she was.

Time is supposed to heal all, but her feelings were mixed. Yes, she had called him and asked him to pick her up at the ferry, and yes, he had risked his life to save her when Andy McDowell had tried to kill her. That last morsel allowed her to cut him some slack.

The deckhand handed her the cat carrier. The grey Persian cat yowled in displeasure.

"It's alright, Percy, we'll be home soon."

The cat purred briefly and stuck a paw through the grate.

"Hello, hello, hello," Archie shouted jauntily in his best English accent as he sauntered across the swaying deck. "I am so glad you called me, Vi."

"Well, I didn't fancy having to lug my bags up to the cottage myself and I thought a cup of tea with you and Gertrude might help me recover from the long trip," Vi responded happily.

The deckhand deposited the last of three satchels filled with food beside the two large suitcases he had already placed on the deck. He waved a greeting to Archie and then disappeared back onto the passenger ferry.

"Nothing like a good cup'a tea between friends," he agreed,

offering Vi his hand. "Hello, Percival, good to see you too."

The cat purred loudly when Archie stroked his outstretched paw.

"Where's Gert, I thought she'd be with you," Vi said, wrapping an arm beneath one of his to steady herself. She looked past him to the empty truck bed.

Archie took the cat crate from her.

"Oh, well that's a bit of a story. How about I load up all your bags and groceries and we stop in at the pub for a burger and a pint before I take you home? I've already started up the woodstove in the cottage, but it is cold in there and it will take a while to warm up."

"I hadn't thought of that. Thank you," Vi responded. "I think a pint and a burger will do just fine."

"And don't you worry, I'll protect you from all the gossipers," he charmed her.

Vi chuckled.

"Are you sure we won't be creating more," she queried.

"Truth be told, I expect we will," he replied with a laugh.

Archie escorted Vi to his truck. She and Percival waited inside the truck until he finished loading the groceries and her suitcases into the truck bed. She wondered what he had to tell her about Gertrude and hoped it wasn't grievous news. Surely Betty would have called her if something had happened to the island's favorite pig.

"There we go," Archie sang as he clambered into the driver's seat. He closed the door and started the engine.

"You know, we could just walk to the pub from here. It's only about a hundred paces," Vi remarked. "I'm not that old."

"Neither am I, but why walk when we can burn a few dinosaurs and arrive in style."

Vi burst out laughing. Tears threatened to spill. She didn't think that 'arriving in style' was a wounded old war horse of a Dodge pickup truck, but then she was on Seal Island where cars were few and limos were non-existent.

Archie grinned and pulled the truck out of its current spot

only to park it ten spots further along, right in front of the pub's steps. He then raced around the side of the truck and held the door open for Vi.

Vi gave him her hand, holding it out as if she were the Queen herself. Archie bowed chivalrously.

"Don't worry, Percy, we won't be long and then you can have a romp in the garden," Archie purred to the cat.

The cat yowled piteously.

Archie and Vi grinned like school kids as they entered the pub, all eyes upon them.

Vi felt all her trepidation at returning to Seal Island vanish as a hearty set of cheers echoed off the walls from the couple of dozen patrons sitting at the bar and at tables around the homey pub.

Stew sat them at a quiet table by the window.

"Good to see you, your Honor," Stew said, wiping off the table.

"Heavens, Stew, don't be so formal," she chided the red-faced pub owner. "Please call me Vi."

"Well, you know we had some words the last time we spoke, and I didn't know if you were still mad at me," he whispered in her ear.

"No, Stew, that's all water under the bridge after all this time," Vi lied. Stew Mann was as slick as a used car salesman and a world class Shylock in Vi's opinion. She would never trust the man but forgive and forget as the saying goes was her motto.

"Two pints and two burgers," Archie chimed in. "We need something to warm us up."

"Cheese and bacon, Vi," Stew asked.

"Why not live a little," the wizened judge agreed. "And a few fried onions too please."

"Oooh, living dangerously, good for you," Stew joked. "The usual, Archie?"

"Yep, just hold the relish," the old man agreed.

Stew left and returned before Vi asked Archie about Gertrude. She wondered how Peaches was doing too after Betty had told her about the cow being tasered.

Stew deposited two mugs of frothy ale on the table in front of them, and then with a wink and a grin, he waddled back to the bar, the bar rag flung over his shoulder.

"So, I have to ask, what made you change your mind about selling," Archie asked as soon as Stew was out of ear shot.

Vi could hear the hopeful tone in his voice as he regarded her with grey-blue eyes, his silver hair slicked back, his bushy eyebrows standing to attention. She almost laughed at the little boy look that had crept over his face... almost.

Again, that niggling feeling troubled her: was that the look he used on Tiffany and her dear sister-in-law, Eliza?

Vi chided herself for letting her imagination run away with her.

"Bone's Bailiwick is my last genuine connection to my brother and Eliza. I won't have the specter of Eliza's death or Andy's terrible assault on me, and you and Betty, destroy my wonderful memories there."

Archie sat back, his mouth twitching, his eyes glinting with mischief.

"What," Vi demanded, not liking the look he gave her.

"You're a feisty little pit-bull, aren't you," he crooned. "I don't mean that in a bad way so don't get mad at me. It's just that you reminded me of my daughter just then. When she sets her mind on something, all the villains in the Marvel Universe couldn't change it."

Vi chuckled.

"And which superhero do you imagine me to be," she asked, lowering her guard.

"I'm not answering that on the grounds...," Archie stammered.

"That it might incriminate you," Vi finished.

They both laughed.

"Tell me," Vi continued, "what's happened with the indomitable Gertrude? She isn't sick, I hope."

"Nah, nothing like that," Archie responded. "Like I said, my daughter's just as feisty as you. Despite my objections, Betty's gone and moved her things into Andy's place, which is hers now. I had Rainbow McDonald in to talk to Peaches because Peaches hasn't been right since she got tasered by that bozo detective. Rainbow and her husband, Frank, they bought Summer's farm and are turning it into some fancy poultry place."

Vi sipped her beer. This sounded like it would be a long story.

"Rainbow's a pet psychic and a good one at that. She says that Peaches was home sick," Archie continued.

Vi listened to Archie regale her with the story of Rainbow and Peaches, Betty's move, and Gertrude's deciding to stay with Betty and Peaches at Andy's old house for now. Vi looked around the room as the assortment of fishermen, hobby farmers, and artists, all chatted amiably together. It gave her a warm feeling to be part of a community like this.

She realized that everything seemed so normal. It was almost as if the bizarre deaths of Eliza, Tiffany and Summer as well as Andy's tragic fall to his demise, had never happened. In some ways that heartened her, in others, it tore at her heart. Was Seal Island so effervescent that the passing of those who lived upon it was simply a blimp in time or was the spell the island cast upon the populace an illusion so great that death, no matter how bizarre, was happenstance and accepted as the norm?

Perhaps Vi wasn't being fair? Life goes on and the tragedies that had struck the island were over a year ago.

The burgers arrived and the pair of them dived into them. Vi had forgotten what an amazing burger the pub served up. Her stomach gurgled in anticipation.

After a time, Archie excused himself and headed off to the little boy's room to do what little boy's do when Stew approached her. He looked around and then bent towards her, picking up the dirty plates as he did so.

"You need to be careful, Judge," he whispered.

"What do you mean," she asked, affronted.

"You're a nice lady and I'd hate to see something happen to ya," Stew hissed.

"Is that a threat," Vi growled, her voice rising.

"Shhhhh, there are too many ears listening in here," he barked, and then lowered his voice once again.

"All I'm saying is that I think you and Betty were right, that Tiff, God rest her soul, was murdered. I dunno about your sister-in-law and that Rivers girl, but everyone knew how allergic Tiff was to peanuts, and that includes her beau. I really cared for that girl. Hell, if she asked me, I'd have left Gwen for her," he confessed. "Maybe she would have if'n she hadn't a fallen for Betty's ex. Who knows?"

Vi gasped, the hair on the back of her neck rising. Stew Mann had fallen in love with Tiffany Hyde-White, mystery writer, Realtor, and sex addict, and perhaps still was? Words couldn't describe the images that flooded into her mind.

Two men exchanged insults about the Canucks and the opposing hockey team battling it out on the television above the bar. Chairs flew into the air.

Gwen Mann, all five foot two of her, slammed a baseball bat on the counter.

"Pay and get out now," the tiny Malaysian woman screamed at them. "Come back tomorrow when you're okay-okie-dokie. Got it?"

The two drunks flinched.

They shoved their hands inside their pockets, pulled out some bills, and threw them on the counter.

Gwen waved the bat around and pointed from one to the other.

The men put a few more bills on the counter and staggered towards the door.

"Like I said, you keep your eyes open and your opinions about the goings on around here to yourself, just like I do," Stew mumbled, standing up.

"You heard my wife, get," he ordered the drunks even though they had already left the pub.

Vi was flabbergasted. She didn't think she could be more so until Archie returned to the table with Barney and his wife, Camille, in tow.

"Good to see you, Vi," Barney said amiably, straddling a chair.

"And you, Barney," Vi replied casually.

Camille said nothing. She simply glared at Violet.

Vi refused to be intimidated and glared right back.

Archie sat down and ordered a round of ales, unaware of the animosity brewing between the two women.

Barney sat back in his chair and laughed uproariously.

"What? What did I miss," Archie exclaimed.

"I am sorry, Judge Bone, but it appears as if my lovely wife hasn't forgiven you for not selling your cottage to her," Barney said, raising his glass to Vi.

"You mean to you," Vi quipped.

"No, to her," Barney replied.

Vi would not be bated, not by Barney Whyte or his perfectly put together trophy wife.

"Apparently my money wasn't good enough," Camille smirked. "And our offer was worth far more than that drafty old cottage was."

Vi glowered. Archie had already told her what Camille's plans had been for Bone's Bailiwick and she was having none of it.

"There's nothing drafty about Vi's cottage, it just needed the woodstove lit," Archie chimed in, breaking the tense moment.

Vi smiled and placed a hand over his.

"Right you are, my friend," Vi responded.

"Still," Camille sniffed, "you could have countered the offer."

"I had already decided that I listed the property too hastily, Mrs. Whyte. It wasn't personal," Vi countered.

"I'm sure it wasn't, Vi," Barney said, realizing the need to placate his wife more than Vi. "You must remember, my dear, that Vi's brother built the cottage with his own bare hands, so it has sentimental value to her."

"No matter," Camille waved her husband off. "One day you'll die, and I'll get what I want, anyway. It's only a matter of time."

A stunned silence met Camille's words.

Stew arrived just in time with three mugs of ale and an enormous glass of Chablis for Camille.

"Here you go, mates," Stew said cheerily, the tenseness around the table not lost on him.

"Thank you, kind sir," Barney replied effusively. "How about a round of the good stuff to go with it, if you know what I mean?"

"Too many people in the pub right now, Barney," Stew mumbled. "I'd lose my liquor license. How about a shot of Irish Whiskey instead?"

"Works for me, my man," Barney joked.

The pub owner spun on his heel, all but running to get away from the tension that had settled like a thunder cloud around the people sitting at the table.

Archie cleared his throat.

"Well, I think we'll just finish up. Vi and her cat have had a tiring day and I'm sure they are exhausted," Archie said, looking pointedly at Vi. "I expect Percival is screaming blue murder by now."

"I am exhausted, Archie, and you're probably right about Percy," Vi agreed. She smiled across the table at him.

Barney and Archie stood up together as Vi rose from her seat.

Camille sipped her wine and simmered.

Barney looked at Vi and shrugged helplessly.

Vi didn't buy it. She knew Camille's type: shrewd, ruthless, spoiled, a woman not to be taken lightly.

For the briefest of moments, Vi wondered just how far Camille would go to get what she wanted and just how far she had gone to nab Barney. The thought was as unsettling as Stew Mann's earlier comments.

Vi's nerves jingled. She was happy to be going and disappointed that she had let Barney and Camille Whyte ruin her return to Seal Island.

"You'll have to let us know what Bet and Reggie find in their Gulliver travels today, Arch," Barney shouted as Archie escorted Vi to the bar.

Archie waved a hand over his head in answer.

"What's he talking about," Vi asked quietly.

"Betty hired Reggie and his boat. They are off cruising. Official business, you know. She's trying to figure out where that severed foot may have come from. Reggie is one of the most skilled mariners that I know. She's in expert hands. If anyone can help her, it'd be our Reg," Archie murmured as he paid their tab. "I wish Barney would shut up about it though."

"I do too," Vi whispered back.

Vi shivered.

Vi had thought that was Reggie's boat she saw leaving the harbor when the ferry pulled in.

The judge was glad that Betty had taken their phone conversation about Tiffany's book to heart. She couldn't wait to hear if Tiffany's strange solving of the severed feet cases could have some truth in it. Vi also couldn't wait to hear Betty's take on Stew Mann's confession.

Vi idly wondered if she also shouldn't mention Camille. There was something nasty about that woman, despite the perfectly highlighted hair and manicured nails. After all, hadn't Barney had a fling with Tiffany too?

It seemed to Vi that if she and Betty could solve Tiffany's murder, they might be able to shed some light on Eliza's and Summer's deaths as well. She was ready to dive back into the cases, safety be damned. She was angry.

Vi grinned, a mischievous glint in her eyes. She hadn't been this fired up since Eliza's funeral.

"Penny for your thoughts," Archie asked as he opened the door for her.

"I was just thinking how lovely it will be to sit by the fire with my cat on my lap and a hot cup of tea," Vi replied smoothly.

"Would you like some company other than the cat," he queried hopefully.

"Not this minute. I'd like to get settled in first," she answered truthfully. "Call me later though."

"I'll do that," he said, perking up.

Archie escorted the judge to the waiting truck where Percival was raising Hell.

Channeling Mazie

A steaming pot of Jasmine tea rested on an old pine table between the two women who sat in overstuffed leather chairs in front of a cast iron woodstove, their faces ruddy from the heat. A painting of an English hunt scene overlooked the two women. Red-coated men with black top hats galloped across a meadow, hounds at their heels, horses elevated and sweat soaked, galloping in pursuit of a quarry that they would never catch.

The two women, one tiny and wizened with age, her white hair neatly fashioned in a short bob, and the other, middle-aged, cinnamon blond hair tinged with white loose about her face and shoulders, watched the fire crackle inside the woodstove.

Behind the chairs, on a dog bed, lay a grey and white pot-bellied pig, her eyes closed. A series of un-ladylike snores shattered the peaceful moment.

"You know, Betty," Vi confessed, "when I returned to Seal Island, I was prepared to let Eliza's spirit rest in peace and move on, away from the sordid details of Eliza, Tiffany and Summer's passing. I started reading Tiffany's detective series last year and found them so amusing that I was hooked. When I read *The Dastardly Mr. Deeds*, it struck a chord. I knew that I had to get you to read it, and here we are."

"Here we are," Betty agreed, "sitting by the fire discussing zombies and murder."

The two women grinned, firelight dancing in their eyes. The pig slept on.

"It seems apparent that you are going to have to go undercover at Angel's Heavenly Gate in the same way that Mazie

Owen did. Life imitating art as they say."

"Yes, I don't know who coined that quote, but it is accurate," Betty agreed, "although, I don't expect to meet any zombie killing undertakers."

Betty sipped her tea and closed her eyes for a moment, relishing the sweet taste of the Jasmine and honey on her tongue.

"I do hope not," Vi replied, and then chuckled.

Betty sighed wearily.

"Be careful, won't you, Vi," Betty added. "From what you told me happened at the pub this afternoon, Stew Mann may know more than he said. I don't like how he approached you and am not surprised that you felt threatened. His confession of being in love with Tiffany, when I look back on it, isn't a total surprise. I don't expect Gwen would have taken his affair lying down. Tiffany's book, however strange, linking the severed feet with a crooked undertaker, and her penchant for sleeping with married men, probably angered a lot of folks. It may even have led to her death, whether it was by the hand of a jealous wife or a shyster remains to be determined. I think I need to have a chat with Tom Powder and ask him to run background checks on Gwen Mann and Camille Whyte. I daren't do it myself."

"I agree, keep your distance from the actual ongoing investigation. You can't risk losing your pension now."

"True," Betty nodded, "I can't. I also can't sit by and let someone get away with murder. One of these women may have killed Tiffany. Jealousy and greed are prime motives. This might solve Tiffany's demise, but it doesn't explain Summer or our dear Eliza's deaths, unless Eliza knew about the affairs and confronted the men. If she did, we could have a motive there as well."

"It would absolve Andy," Vi said pointedly.

"It would. I still can't fathom why he did what he did or why he would confess to something he didn't do," Betty murmured. "It was so out of the blue and out of character."

"And you haven't found any clues in your new home," Vi

queried.

"Not a one. No drugs. No hidden cupboards or hiding places. Even the lead poisoning is a puzzle. Doc Forester told me it was ongoing so some of it was probably from the old copper pipes, but there were signs of recent poisoning too. The lab tested everything they could think of in the house and it all came up clean," Betty said, puzzled.

"And you feel comfortable there?"

"Yes, surprisingly," Betty said. "Like you do here, I expect. I have nothing but wonderful memories in that house, both of Andy and his mother."

Betty picked up the tea pot and topped up their cups of tea.

"It appears we are back on the case regardless," Vi mused.

"It appears so," Betty murmured.

***

Tom Powder sat in his office reviewing case files. His partner, Inspector Ben Hammerton, was on holidays for two weeks. He liked his young protégé, but Powder had to admit that he was enjoying the sound of silence from the desk across from his work cubicle.

The telephone rang beside him.

"Chief Inspector Tom Powder," he said, answering the call.

Powder's eyebrows knit together as he listened to Sergeant Betty Bruce discuss the goings-on on Seal Island as well as her conversation with Judge Violet Bone.

Powder picked up a pen and scrawled on a scratch pad: Gwen Mann, Malaysian, about 25–30 years of age, and Camille Whyte, US citizen, fortyish, wife of Barney Whyte, billionaire.

Tom whistled under his breath. He would have to tread carefully in looking into Barney Whyte's dealings. He had already been warned about him, not just by Betty earlier, but by his superiors prior to taking on the Seal Island cases.

"So, you think that Tiffany Hyde-White's case, out of the three, was a murder and not an accident," he asked Betty. "That'll piss off the family. They got a hefty settlement from the chocolate manufacturers."

Tom swiveled in his office chair and stared at the clouds outside the window, listening thoughtfully to what Betty was saying. Suddenly, he sat up straighter and laughed.

"Are you serious? A crooked undertaker," he gasped. "And you actually found a real cemetery that matches the description from one of our dead lady's books? Remind me never to get on your bad side."

Powder made some more notes.

"Hey, I know that I'm not on your task force, but I'd like to join you on your trip to Lund. I haven't been undercover for a while," he said, his chair squeaking as he leaned back in it.

"Great. I'll be on the next boat," he said happily. "I'll pick you up on the big island we'll head up island to the Powell River ferry."

Powder grinned as he hung up the phone.

***

Betty and Tom pulled into the parking lot of the Angel's Heavenly Gate Funeral Home just outside of the tiny town of Lund, just north of Powell River on the British Columbia coast.

The morning fog was lifting, and it threatened to be a sunny day. Both Betty and Tom had commented on the ferry from Vancouver Island to Powell River that it had been so long since they had seen the sun that they had forgotten what it looked like.

Betty and Tom dressed down for the day. Betty wore a pale pink sweater and blue jeans, Tom a black leather jacket and black jeans.

They had practiced their speech in the car: Betty's mother had just died, and her mother's wishes were to be buried some place by the sea. The simpler the story, the easier to pull off, they had agreed.

They stepped out of the car and looked up at the small

weathered clap-board chapel located next to the sprawling newer building which housed the office, boardroom, and chapel which made up the Angel's Heavenly Gate Funeral Home. All the buildings needed repair and a coat of paint.

"There's nothing angelic about this place," Powder said.

"Except for the ocean views, it is dismal, isn't it," Betty agreed.

The sparkling blue ocean at the end of the property made a pretty backdrop for the ancient cemetery. Most of the stones were old and moss covered, but some were new, the granite faces shiny and moist with dew.

"Time to put on your grieving daughter game face," the inspector said.

Betty pulled a tiny vial of apple cider vinegar from her pocket. She took a sniff of the pungent liquid. Her eyes watered instantly.

"Here I was ready to tweak your pretty apple dumpling cheeks," Power joked.

"Very funny," she quipped.

Powder grinned and offered her his arm.

Betty placed the vial back in her jean's pocket and pulled out a Kleenex. She sniffed and accepted his arm, a sly smile quickening on her face.

The pair climbed up the steps and opened the door to the office.

"How may I help you," a pinched spinster of a woman asked from behind the tall reception desk. Beyond her were rows of grey steel file cabinets and a worn metal desk that looked like it came from an office surplus store.

"My wife just lost her mother," Tom replied, wrapping an arm protectively around Betty's shoulder. "We've tried everywhere to find a place where we can bury her beside the ocean. Those were her final wishes and we want to honor them. One of the funeral home directors we talked to recommended you to us."

Betty was pleased by how well her impromptu partner lied.

"Well, we usually only take locals, but I'll call Mr. Whitaker," she grumbled, picking up the handle of a black telephone. She dialed an extension and listened to it ring.

Betty cuddled close to Tom Powder and did her best to look both stricken and hopeful at the same time.

"Mr. Whitaker, there are some folks at the front to see you," the woman grumbled.

"He'll be here in a moment," she said, hanging up.

A rakish man in his late thirties dressed in a charcoal grey Armani suit, spit polished black shoes, and sporting a diamond studded Gucci watch, appeared from out of a hidden door somewhere at the back of the office.

Powder and Betty exchanged an amused glance. Who wears watches anymore?

"How may I help you," the boyish man asked. His voice was soft and elegant. "My name is Brian Whitaker. I am the Funeral Director here."

"I'm looking for a plot for my mother," Betty blurted out.

"With a sea view," the secretary cut in rudely.

"My mother-in-law's wishes were to be buried by the sea. Despite living on the coast, we have discovered that is a hard thing to do," Powder added.

"It is indeed," Whitaker agreed. "Well I am sure we can help you."

"Oh, thank you," Betty sobbed. She dabbed at her eyes. "I didn't think we would be able to do it."

Whitaker walked around the counter and smiled at Betty and Tom.

"Let me show you around first," he offered, leading the way out of the office and to the chapel.

"We have a lovely prayer chapel that is available for small services as well as a board room where we cater to larger family and friend gatherings."

"Oh, my mum was ninety-seven," Betty gushed. "All of her friends are long gone, I'm afraid, and I'm her only daughter.

"We just want to do right by her," Powder said, stepping forward.

"Ah, I see," Whitaker replied smoothly. "May I ask if your

mother has, um, already been prepared for burial and if you have already chosen a casket?"

"Yes," answered Betty.

"No," Powder responded at the same time.

"What my husband means to say is that 'yes' my mother is currently resting at another funeral home that we had originally chosen before we found a letter she had left with her final wishes."

"We haven't chosen a casket yet," Tom lied outright.

"Then let me escort you to the side office where we have a variety of caskets to choose from and then I'll take you out onto the grounds and show you the plots we have available. There is one in particular I think your mother..." Whitaker responded, extending a hand and pointing back towards the main building.

"Edith," Betty sniffed. "Edith Beale."

"That your mother, Mrs. Beale, would have loved," Whitaker continued.

"So far so good," Tom whispered in Betty's ear as they followed Brian Whitaker to the casket display area.

Both Tom and Betty did a double take when they entered the room. There were a dozen unique styles and finishes on the caskets before them, but the one thing that they all had in common was that they were all about sixty inches long instead of the usual eighty-three inches.

"My, they are lovely," Betty exclaimed.

"And a tad short," Tom chimed in.

"My mother is quite tall," Betty said worriedly, staying true to her role."

"Oh, these are just display models," the Funeral Director stated, and then chuckled as if sharing a joke with them.

"That makes sense," Tom agreed, the timbre in his voice indicating to Betty that it didn't, really.

"I do like this walnut one, honey, what do you think?"

"Sure, sweetie, I think Mom would like that, but look at that polished copper metal one. That's slick."

"Yes, we carry traditional wood finish and metal coffins,"

Whitaker crooned, "but the walnut finish is my favorite too. It's a marvelous choice; it's one of our most elite caskets. I am sure if Mrs. Beale were here, she would love it too."

"I still like the copper," Tom quipped.

Betty rolled her eyes at him. One would think they were actually married, they disagreed so well.

Whitaker then showed them his most exclusive line of gravestones including white marble and cultured sandstone, or so he called it. There were all different sizes from plaques to three-foot-tall slabs of stone.

"Oh, I think the marble. The largest one you have. That way we can see her grave from the water when we go boating," Tom said, his voice warbling.

Betty stifled a laugh with a sob.

"May we go for a tour of the cemetery now," Betty croaked. "I'm finding it a little close in here."

"Definitely. I am sure this is overwhelming," Whitaker said. "Have I told you that the cemetery and chapel have been in my family for over a hundred and fifty years? The 'Angel' in Angel's Heavenly Gate was my great grandmother's sister's name."

"Oh, really," Betty replied, fascinated as the three of them strolled the acreage.

Betty had to admit the view was spectacular. She could see all the way to the inland mountains of Vancouver Island from the top of the rise.

"What happened to her," she asked casually.

"My grandmother told me she ran away with a ship's captain. It's quite a romantic story, eloping off to sea with a handsome navy man. My grandmother said that her father tried to have her sister interred here when she died of cholera in England many years later, but her husband wouldn't allow it. My great-grandfather named the chapel after her."

"That is quite the family history," Tom agreed.

Betty saw Tom Powder smirk. His ancestors went back thousands of years on the coast. She could tell he was biting back a reply.

Whitaker's story put the myth of the sea casting Angel's body back into her murderous father's lap via the Glory Hole to bed. That reminded her though that she needed to get a better look at the blowhole from here.

Betty ambled farther into the cemetery toward the cliff edge as Tom steered the Funeral Director farther away towards the empty plot on the far side of the cemetery that Whitaker wanted to sell them.

She knew she shouldn't venture too close to the edge, but the sight of the sea spray exploding in a rainbow of color above the Glory Hole was dazzling.

Just like in Tiffany's novel, the cemetery's fence line ended a few feet away from the cliff top and a crater in the ground beside one of the old gravesites looked deep enough that it may well be the opening to an underground cave.

Betty stood mulling that last bit over when she heard a commotion behind her.

"Get back," Whitaker screamed as he raced towards her, Tom Powder following behind at a much more leisurely pace.

"That's dangerous. The cliff underneath there is unstable," he cried out.

"Oh," Betty feigned surprise.

Whitaker skidded to a stop in his slick Italian leather shoes. Betty noticed that the leather would need quite the polishing to restore it to its previous luster.

He reached for Betty.

Betty took grasped his outstretched hand and smiled demurely back at him.

Powder sauntered towards his fake wife, not quite able to hide the grin on this face.

"I told Mr. Whitaker here that we have to head back home, but you and I will talk it over and call him tomorrow," Powder advised her.

"Oh, okay, dear, if you think that's best," she replied.

"I like to sleep on things before we make any big decisions," Powder purred.

Whitaker's eyes glittered with what Betty assumed was greed but could easily have been menace as well.

"That would be fine, Mister... ah, I am sorry, I don't believe I asked you your names," Whitaker stuttered apologetically.

"Horse-Afraid," Tom said, "Benjamin and Doris Horse-Afraid.

The Funeral Director shook hands with Mr. and Mrs. Horse-Afraid.

"That's an interesting name," Whitaker said, almost grinding his teeth as he did so.

"Yep, you think you got stories about your family, you should hear mine," quipped Tom.

"I can just imagine," Whitaker growled, and then turned back on the charm. "I expect your family history makes ours pale in comparison, doesn't it, Mrs. Horse-Afraid, or may I call you Doris?"

"Call me Doris, please," Betty crooned.

"Overall, I think your mum would love that plot, sweetie, but like I said already, we'll sleep on it and call Mr. Whitaker in the morning."

"Okay," Betty squeaked.

Tom reached for Betty's hand and they walked out of the cemetery, Whitaker in his now not so preen Armani suit walking sedately by their side.

Whitaker handed Tom his business card in the parking lot and waved a goodbye as he entered the building.

"What do you think," Powder asked his new partner. "You think those tiny coffins are just display models like he said?"

"I think we're coming back with a warrant and a dive team," Betty responded.

"It's going to be hard to prove," Powder cautioned her.

"Maybe, maybe not," she replied earnestly. "And where did Benjamin and Doris Horse-Afraid come from, anyway?"

"A Blackfoot buddy of mine's name is Horse-Afraid. It's a good name."

"And Doris?"

"I dunno, I just thought you looked like you could be a Doris."

Betty grimaced as she got into the car.

Powder chuckled.

Betty punched him in the arm as he sat down in the driver's seat beside her.

"Ouch, that hurt."

"You can call me anything, but…," she started.

"Late for breakfast," Tom joked.

"Don't ever call me Doris again."

"Does that mean we aren't burying your mother here?"

Betty laughed.

Powder joined in.

"I can't wait to see the look on the Superintendent's face when you ask him for a warrant to search the Angel's Gate Heavenly Funeral Home and Cemetery," Powder guffawed.

Severed Relations

Tom and Betty sat together inside the downtown office of the RCMP, working in the boardroom. They sat typing at their computers, researching cases involving murder or fraudulent goings on at funeral homes.

"Here's a good case precedent," Powder said, pushing his screen towards her.

"Martin Bell was charged with fraud and desecrating a body after he cut the feet off one Reginald Winston Garner to make the body fit inside a standard-sized casket. Mr. Garner was a former basketball player with the NBA. The coroner ruled his death an accidental overdose until they discovered his wife had an extra two-million-dollar life insurance policy on him and was having an affair with his agent. The desecration was discovered when they exhumed the body for further testing."

"You don't think...," Betty muttered.

"That our undertaker, Mr. Brian Whitaker, is cutting the feet off the cadavers before he buries them to make them fit in his tiny caskets," Powder finished. "I bet those pint-sized coffins cost him way less than normal ones. Heck, I bet they were cast-offs, and he bought them in bulk."

"But why throw the severed feet into the salt chuck," Betty burst out, her brain whirring. "Why not just toss them in the coffin and bury the evidence?"

"Maybe the guy's got a foot fetish," Tom suggested.

"And who do you know who buries a loved one with sneakers on their feet," Betty asked him.

"And how in Hell do we get a warrant to dig up a grave to see if the occupant's feet are sawed off," he returned.

"First things first," Betty said with gusto, "we get a warrant to search the cliff and underground cave stating probable cause that some of our feet came from bodies inside coffins within unsafe gravesites that were tumbling into the water. That alone would get the knickers in a twist of the Ministry of Environment boys and girls."

Powder grinned.

"You are so devious, Sergeant Bruce. Sure, get the environmentalists all fired up."

"Once we find our evidence, which I'm sure we will, we expand the warrant. If we don't find one single regular sized coffin anywhere on that property, and we can find one family with a loved one there willing to let us exhume a body, we'll get a judge to issue a blanket warrant."

"It was the Armani suit that did it for you, wasn't it," Powder asked, charmed by Betty's determination.

"Yep. What kind of Funeral Director of some backwater falling down chapel and cemetery has the money to buy Armani and Gucci unless they are skimming the books or found a way to stiff the stiffs," she said exuberantly.

"I hope my partner takes an extended vacation. Working with you is the bomb, as my daughter would say," Powder said, slamming the palm of his hand down on the table. "Let's go find us the big kahuna and organize a posse with scuba gear."

***

Betty, Tom, three members of her team, and one environmental protection officer, stood on the deck of the police boat watching two members of the police dive team suit up. The water slurped against the sides of the cruiser as it rocked slowly in a southern breeze. Gulls rode the currents, trilling above the gunwales of the boat, looking for handouts.

They couldn't have wished for a nicer day. It was balmy and only required light windbreakers. The sun beating down on the water and the men and women on deck was a welcome embrace after the five months of incessant rain and storms they had just experienced.

The tide was high. Deep blue green water gently rolled in and splashed against the giant rocks at the base of the cliff. Turbidity in the water was low, so the divers had good visibility.

The blowhole, or Glory Hole, as Reggie Phoenix had called it, was docile today, but everyone on board the cruiser knew that the situation could change in minutes on the west coast.

The divers gave Betty and the captain of the cruiser a thumbs-up as they dropped backwards off the boat into the salt water.

Betty let out the breath she hadn't realized she was holding.

"This is going to be interesting," the guy from the Ministry of Environment said.

"That's an understatement," Powder commented dryly.

"What I'm referring to is the paperwork mess this will cause on jurisdictional issues if in fact there are caskets and bodies down there," the pink-cheeked young environmental officer added, pointing to the cliff top where a triangular piece of something poked out of the sandstone cliff face. "And by the looks of that indent in the cliff up there, and what looks like the edge of a coffin sticking out of it, I think that is a given."

Betty gasped. There was a paragraph in Tiffany's book that described the exact thing. She wondered if that was one of the things that Tiffany had wanted to talk to her about the night she died in the snow amongst her garden gnomes.

"Maybe we'll luck out," one of Betty's team members said, "and the divers will find a severed foot wedged under a rock down there."

Everyone standing on deck laughed.

The small group watched in anticipation as twin lines of oxygen bubbles bursting on the surface of the water marked the progress of the two members of the dive team beneath the waves.

They waited… and they waited.

"Tide's going to turn in about half an hour," the captain said. "They'll have to come out of the water by then. The current will get too strong for them, especially here where that point opens up into the inlet."

Betty nodded, barely listening.

Tom Powder chewed on the cuticle of his right index finger.

The environmental officer leaned on the railing; his gaze focused downwards, the light breeze lifting his brown hair into a Mohawk.

The three members of Betty's special project team drank coffee and paced the deck.

Finally, one of the diver's came up. He lifted his mask and removed the breathing apparatus from his mouth.

"We got caskets. We've counted seven so far. There are some pretty messed up bodies inside two of them and a few empty ones that broke into pieces when they hit the ground," the diver called up to Betty.

"Any of them missing feet," Tom Powder yelled.

"There are all sorts of missing body parts. Given the clothes on one corpse, I'd say these are old bodies, but I'm no expert," the diver replied. "The bodies from inside the busted coffins are probably long gone. My partner is still checking a few things out."

"Do any of those coffins look new or anything odd about them you can see," Powder added.

"I don't think so, but it will take more than two of us to locate everything that's fallen down from that cliff. As far as 'odd', it's frigging surreal down there, right out of a horror movie, only in Technicolor. I've never seen anything like it."

"Can you see an entrance to an underground cave at all," Betty asked. "From up top, there looks like there might be a cave under there somewhere."

"That's what Dave is checking out. He can't go in though. It's too dangerous," the diver answered. "I gotta go back down."

Betty waved at him.

The diver washed out his mask and put his mouthpiece back in before descending to the depths once again.

"Well, this is a pickle, isn't it," the environmental officer said.

"Yep, but it gives us enough to get a warrant," Betty drawled.

"It will that," Powder agreed.

Betty and her crew high-fived each other.

"With any luck, we'll get the right judge to give us a blanket warrant," Powder said, leaning over the railing.

"I'll put on my best uniform," Betty joked.

***

The people in the town of Lund didn't know what hit them as a lengthy line of police vehicles, vans and SUV's, as well as two Ministry of Environment and Ministry of Oceans & Fisheries trucks, sped through town. Five police cruisers, four unmarked SUVs, and three forensic teams. How they kept this a secret from the press was anyone's guess. Betty suspected it would quickly become a feeding frenzy for the media as person after person yanked out their cell phones and started recording.

Betty arrived at the Angel's Gate Heavenly Funeral Home and Cemetery with a full entourage in tow. She was in the first SUV along with the Superintendent himself. The superintendent had joined the expedition but had agreed that Betty should take the lead.

Betty regretted that Tom Powder wasn't with them. He had another case that took precedent.

Betty and her boss entered the front office, both dressed in full uniform. In fact, all the men and women, except for the forensic teams and Doc Forester, wore crisp uniforms, and had polished their boots to a shine Betty was sure could be seen from the space station.

The old spinster secretary sitting behind the counter looked ready to have a heart attack.

"Mr. Whitaker if you please," Betty said, slamming the warrant down on top of the counter.

There were no scowls or ill remarks this time, Betty noted. The secretary, face warped by bitterness, lifted the phone to page Brian Whitaker, but he stepped out of the side office before she could do so.

Whitaker's face turned ashen.

He wore a charcoal fitted suit, paisley tie, and crisp white dress shirt.

"Can I help you," he stammered.

"Mr. Whitaker, this is a blanket warrant which gives us the right to search all the grounds and these premises," Betty stated, standing tall.

"Mrs. Horse-Afraid... I don't understand," Whitaker gasped, puzzled.

The superintendent chuckled.

"It's not Doris Horse-Afraid, Mr. Whitaker, its Sergeant Beatrice Bruce, RCMP," she said resolutely. "We've found evidence of bodies and caskets in the water at the bottom of the blowhole. That, of course, should have been reported to the police and the Ministry of the Environment and the Department of Fisheries, and several other ministries it seems, quite some time ago. We have a blanket warrant to search for more improper disposal of human remains. That is a criminal offense."

"I told you you'd get your come-uppance one day," the secretary hissed.

"Shut up, Pearl," Whitaker growled at her.

"Officer Gantry will stay with you," Betty said to the nasty woman. "Officer Gantry will read you your rights. If you wish to make a statement, you can do so, but I urge you to speak to Counsel first."

The officer in question strode by Betty and took his place beside the secretary's desk.

"Please come with us, Mr. Whitaker," the superintendent ordered, motioning two officers behind him forward. "These officers will be your escorts while you take me on a tour."

The superintendent's eyes lit up with glee as he looked down at Betty. He was a bear of a man, six foot four, broad shouldered and narrow of hip. He played rugby in his spare time. Betty would hate to face him on the field. He was a talented leader and the men and women who answered to him were a proud bunch.

Whitaker was visibly shaking as two officers escorted him out of the office and down the hall, the superintendent towering over the wiry Funeral Director.

Doc Forester joined Betty as she walked towards the casket room.

"What on earth are these," Forester stammered when he saw the short coffins for the first time. Despite the beautiful wood grains and polish, it was an odd spectacle.

"Display models according to our illustrious funeral director," she responded.

"There is no such thing as a five-foot tall display model," Forester said. "I haven't seen this in all of my years on the job."

"I've seen ones like these before," one of the techs said, entering the room behind them. "They custom make them in Malaysia and Indonesia. Only Catholics bury their dead in coffins there for the most part. Space is limited."

"You think Whitaker is importing these," Betty asked the forensic tech.

"He'd have to order a whole shipping crate full to make it cost effective, but I suppose he could," the tech agreed. "Did you know that in the States, you can buy a coffin on Amazon? My aunt did. It was a really nice one too."

"Now I've heard everything," Doc Forester said.

"Not quite. Some dude actually put up a review on Amazon that he bought one to nap in at work. He said he loved it; it was uber comfy and quiet. He thought they should have interior lights as an option," the tech added humorously.

"Bet his co-workers weren't amused," Betty groaned.

"Yep, he said that too."

"Maybe this is how he's paying for his spiffy suits," Betty quipped.

"Be hard to fit a regular sized Canadian or American into one of those caskets," Doc Forester said, examining one of the stubby caskets.

"You'd have to saw off the feet to do it, wouldn't you say," Betty asked him?

"And our warrant," Doc Forester mused.

"Is a blanket warrant, and this is...," Betty agreed.

"Probable cause to dispose of caskets and unwanted parts over the cliff, per the initial charge of 'unlawful disposing of human remains'," the coroner agreed.

"Sweet," the tech said.

Further investigation revealed a cardboard box full of discarded shoes including sneakers of various makes and sizes in the embalming room. There were also the embalmers tools of the trade neatly set out on a table beside the single embalming table and then some unexpected ones including a small hand saw. The hand saw seemed incongruous in its slightly rusted state as the rest of the instruments were spotless, and the countertops bleached.

It disappointed Betty that there was nobody prepped for burial missing its feet, but the excited gleam in Doc Forester and his tech's eyes made her think the superintendent would be one happy man by the end of the day.

"Penny for your thoughts, Doc," Betty asked the coroner.

Doc Forester's eyes crinkled, his silver hair shone brightly under the fluorescent lights, as he picked the small hand saw up in his gloved hands and examined the thin serrated blade. A Mona Lisa smile creased his lips.

"If I was a betting man, I would bet my entire month's pay that this saw's blades will match the tool marks on at least two of the ankle bones that we have preserved in the vault," Forester ventured. "And it looks like our Funeral Director doesn't bother to clean all of his tools thoroughly. As I recall, we found metal flakes imbedded in one of the bones."

"If the teeth on that saw are a match for the severed feet, do you think that will be enough to get us an exhumation order on one of the most recently buried bodies," she said, excitedly.

"I am sure that there is a judge out there willing to do so," he responded.

"Press is here," an officer said, poking his head in through the doorway.

"That didn't take long," the coroner commented dryly.

"That's why the big guy is here," Betty responded smoothly. "'No comment' will be the order of the day until you complete your report."

Betty straightened her jacket and her hat before heading for the door. She knew the superintendent would want her by his side for this.

With a spring in her step, she strode outside to the flash of cameras and whirl of video cameras as the superintendent waved her forward. Betty almost burst out laughing as she noticed how hard the superintendent was working at trying to smother the grin on his face.

Representatives from the Ministry of Environment and the Department of Ocean and Fisheries stood awkwardly beside him, both unaccustomed to on-the-spot press conferences.

"All I can tell you, ladies and gentlemen, is that Sergeant Beatrice Bruce is the head of this investigation. We discovered a series of old caskets and human remains in the water at the base of the cliff of the cemetery. That is all I can comment about at this time, but I am sure that these men from the Ministry of the Environment and Fisheries can fill you in on some details."

"Superintendent isn't Sergeant Bruce in charge of the investigation into the severed feet that have washed up on the shores on some of the islands in the gulf," one sharp reporter queried. "Is there a chance that those severed feet came from here?"

"No comment," Betty replied briskly.

"Investigations are still on-going," the superintendent added. "That's all we have to say."

The superintendent escorted Betty back into the funeral home under the watchful eye of several officers.

"Great work," he said to Betty as they walked down the hallway of the funeral home.

"That will depend on Doc Forester's findings," she responded.

"True, but you nailed it, Sergeant Bruce."

"Thank you, Sir, but I had a little help from some friends."

"You mean the pig? Gertrude, is it? I've heard a lot about her. I hear Inspector Hammerton nearly got lynched by a Seal Island mob trying to take a foot away from her."

Betty laughed.

"Actually, Superintendent, Hammerton nearly got lynched because he tasered my father's cow instead of our pig, but, yes, it was Gertrude, an undertaker-slash-zombie killer named Mr. Deeds, a deceased writer, and a duly licensed pot grower-slash-retired fisherman who were instrumental in helping me solve the mystery of the severed feet, not to mention Chief Inspector Powder who came with me to work undercover here."

"Let's keep some of those details between ourselves, shall we," the superintendent replied, amused.

"Yes, Sir," Betty agreed whole heartedly.

***

"I hear you're a hero," Tom Powder said as he wheeled an office chair up beside Betty as she sat at her cubicle filling in paperwork.

"I wouldn't go that far," she beamed, "and I had a lot of help."

"Yep, I polished up my halo before we went undercover," Tom joked.

"Actually, I was referring to Tiffany's book."

"The zombie killing undertaker one?"

"Oh, you've read it," Betty asked, surprised.

"Someone brought a copy into the lunchroom. I read it after I noticed who the author was," Tom admitted.

Betty shook her head in disbelief. No wonder Tom had wanted to join her undercover.

"I can't believe the greed of some people. Cutting off corpse's feet and stuffing them in a tiny coffin to save money," Betty complained.

"Was it true that Whitaker kept reusing the same coffin for viewings and then would switch them out for the stubby model," Tom asked, incredulous.

"Yeah, he confessed after a dozen families called the station demanding that their loved ones be exhumed after they saw the newscast. Sure enough, five of the coffins we dug up had corpses with sawed off feet. Forensics is having a field day matching up the severed feet to the bodies. We'll probably never know how many poor people he did this too. He clammed up after he changed lawyers."

"A little birdie whispered to me you're up for a promotion too."

"Little birdie is wrong," Betty said, sheepishly. "I've had enough. I decided to retire. I've got thirty years on the force."

Tom was surprised.

Betty shrugged.

"Well, before you hang up your red serge completely, how about working with me as a Special Consultant?"

"Oh, why," Betty asked, intrigued.

"I did a little digging on Gwen Mann and Barney and Camille Whyte," he said. He smacked his lips like he'd just tasted something juicy.

"And?"

"And Gwen Mann has a record for assault with a deadly weapon and assault causing bodily harm. She almost killed a girl at a bar because she flirted with her boyfriend. She did three years and got the rest off for good behavior. In other words, they needed the jail cell," Powder grimaced. "This was two years before she married your pub owner."

"Interesting."

"And then we have your illustrious moonshine making billionaire condo factory owner and his delightful wife," Powder said.

"What's the deal there," Betty inquired, leaning forward.

"Mrs. Camille Whyte is as pure as a daisy. Mr. Barney Whyte is another matter. He is under investigation in India for child exploitation and safety code violations at his factories. Forty people died last year, half of whom were under the age of twelve, in a toxic factory fire. The government is threatening to shut down his entire operation if he doesn't commit to fair labor practices and bring in stringent new safety equipment."

"It's always money and sex, Tom," Betty whined. "I've had enough."

"You may have had enough, but it was your friends that died on Seal Island. Do you mean to tell me you don't want to see justice done?"

"You can be a bully, can't you, Chief Inspector Powder," Betty said grumpily, but then she smiled.

"Did you just play me?"

"Hook, line and sinker," Betty winked.

"So… you'll be my consultant? Help me navigate the weird and wonderful world of Seal Island," Powder asked, already knowing the answer.

"Clear it with the big kahuna and I'm in."

"Already done," Powder quipped.

The two laughed.

"Sounds good," Betty replied, leaning back in her chair, her expression darkening. "I'm thinking I might need you to back me up on something I've been contemplating. If I'm not a cop anymore, there's nothing to stop me from shaking a few trees."

"But you be careful, that Gwen Mann really laid a beating on the girl that batted her eyes at her fella, and that Barney Whyte isn't as nice as he lets on," Tom warned her. "If you can find me something to connect the dots, I'd be happy to drag either of them in, but I don't want to be dealing with another bizarre death on Seal Island, especially yours."

"Fair enough," Betty agreed, knowing she would shake things up anyway.

"And by the way," Tom added casually. "My wife informed me that she wants a divorce. It seems she wants to pursue other options."

"What other options," Betty gasped, surprised.

"No idea, but maybe in a few months, since you won't be an officer of the law officially anymore, you'd like to try going for lunch with me again. This time we won't invite the SWAT team."

Betty blushed.

"You don't need to answer right away," Tom back-pedaled after seeing her look of discomfort.

Betty thought about it for a moment. She was flummoxed by his offer: a date with Tom Powder? Huh! He was a nice guy, and he looked positively scrumptious in black jeans and leather.

"I'd love to go for lunch with you sometime, Tom," Betty responded.

Tom grinned.

She grinned back.

"We'll chat soon then," he replied.

Rainbow Stew

Gertrude and Peaches hung out outside the Bristling Boar Pub. Gertrude stared longingly through the pub's windows at the patrons inside. The men and women seated inside by the window laughed and tapped on the windowpane. The pig was not amused.

Gertrude saw movement other than the tapping of fingers on the glass inside the pub. She squealed with delight, her tail whipping around and around in circles.

"Here ya go, my friend," Reggie said, ambling out of the pub and putting a plate of French fries down on the ground for Gertrude.

The pig snorted and dived into the deep-fried potatoes.

"Don't ya worry, I haven't forgotten ya either, Peaches," the grizzled old fisherman chirped, pulling an apple from his pocket.

He handed the golden Delicious apple to the cow.

She carefully took it from his outstretched hand and chewed happily, green foam dripping from her mouth.

Reggie patted the pig and the cow on the head before striding off to the docks, his gait jaunty, and a smile tickling his lips. Betty had moved back to the island permanently, and he was a happy man.

Inside the pub, Vi watched Reggie feed the animals and then stroll away, disappearing onto his boat which was moored halfway up the long dock. She wished he had stayed. She was uncomfortable with the people sitting at her table, all except for Archie, but he was blissfully unaware of her unease.

In some part of her mind, Vi found it amusing that while her last name was Bone, it was Barney's wife, Camille, who had a bone to pick with her. The woman just wouldn't leave well enough alone.

"Right, four hundred thousand is my last offer," Camille stated, her eyes narrowing. "It's more than it's worth, but I am making an allowance for 'sentimental value'."

"I told you, Camille," Vi said, growing weary of the argument, "my cottage is not for sale."

"Enough, Cam. Vi's already told you twice in the last ten minutes that Bone's Bailiwick isn't for sale no matter how much you offer her," Archie growled, placing a comforting hand over Vi's.

Vi smiled weakly at him. She was developing a headache. Camille Whyte was insufferable.

The trophy wife of the billionaire condom factory owner glowered into her fourth glass of wine. She was unaccustomed to not getting what she wanted. Vi had no intention of caving in.

"I don't know why you don't take it," Gwen Mann chimed in. "That's good money. You could buy a posh pad for that, maybe even a young man to come in and look after you. A woman your age, she should have a handsome young man to order around."

Gwen laughed as her husband rolled his eyes at her.

"With that kind of money, I'd trade you in," Gwen joked. "Maybe you'd like to buy our place, Camille?"

"Thank you, but I don't need a dirty old pub," Camille sulked.

"It's not dirty," Gwen retorted.

"And it's not for sale," Stew admonished his wife.

"I was talking about our house anyway," Gwen sulked

Vi ground her teeth. The table full of catty women was driving her mad. She wished Betty were there with them.

"I don't think the Judge needs the money, and that cottage means a lot to her," Stew replied pointedly. "I can't answer the young stud question though."

"Thank you, Stew," Vi said earnestly, and then switched her attention to Gwen. "Hiring a handsome young housekeeper would be nice, Gwen, but the woman I hired to come in once a week is lovely and needs the work."

Gwen smiled at Vi.

"Are you sure? I can ask my cousin to come from Singapore. He's strong and handsome and has nice hands. He'd put a smile on your face, I can assure you of that."

"Over my dead body," Archie burst in.

"That can be arranged too. My cousin will do what he's told to do," Gwen teased Archie.

"Whoa, I think we better change the subject," Stew said boisterously.

Vi noticed Barney studying her across the table. She didn't like the shrewd look she saw in his eyes. He had hardly uttered a word all through dinner.

Vi took a sip of beer and then pushed the glass away. She had the uneasy feeling that she needed to keep her wits about her, even if she was with Archie.

***

Inside what was once Andy McDowell's house, a woman's touch was visible. Fresh flowers graced the kitchen table. Candles filled every space. Brightly colored throw rugs lay scattered on the enormous dark green corduroy couch. The black and white sterile furniture was gone. It was a warm and cozy home again. Even the ghosts had been laid to rest.

Pictures of Betty in uniform graced the walls, and an enormous picture of Gertrude rested on the mantle above the fireplace.

Betty's sunflower yellow raincoat hung in the closet by the front door, as did her winter coats and bomber jackets.

Betty rummaged through the fridge in the kitchen. She pulled out a block of cheddar and cut it into thick strips. She placed them on a plate beside wedges of apple and cantaloupe.

The kettle boiled.

Betty made a coffee and then opened the liquor cabinet.

"That's odd," she mumbled.

Inside the cupboard were several bottles of red and white

wine and a bottle of Bailey's.

"I could have sworn there were a couple of mickies of Barney's home brew in here. It's not like I fancy it very often. Huh!"

Betty shrugged, thinking she must have been mistaken, and took down the bottle of Bailey's. She measured out a shot and poured it into her coffee.

Betty picked up her coffee cup and the plate of cheese and fruit and made her way upstairs. She was looking forward to a quiet evening in. For the first time in over thirty years she didn't have to feel guilty about the mounds of paperwork that needed dealing with at the office. She was looking forward to getting used to that.

Betty went into the den and sat down by the fire upstairs. It was her favorite room. She loved all the books that surrounded her and the view of Watchtower Mountain out the window. It smelled and felt like Andy. It was now comforting instead of daunting.

On the table beside the Lazy Boy in which she sat lay Summer's diary.

Betty placed the coffee cup by the diary, pulled a quilt over her lap, and tucked her feet underneath her.

She popped a piece of cheese into her mouth and then picked up the diary and began to read.

Betty flipped through the pages, skipping some sections, and carefully reading others, a look of incredulity spreading across her face.

She stopped and sipped her coffee.

The sun was setting in the West. Watchtower Mountain's shadow crept over the fields, creating a Medieval landscape as dark as the Middle Ages.

Betty felt a chill creep over her. She turned on the Tiffany lamp on the table beside her and flipped to the back of the diary, to Summer's last entries.

Betty's face turned pale. Her hands trembled.

"Oh, shit! Vi," she swore and scrambled out of the chair.

Betty tore down the stairs and into the kitchen. She ripped the cell phone out of the charger and dialed Vi's cell number.

The phone rang and rang. It finally went to voice mail.

***

In the barn at the McDonald's farm, the heat lamps glowed above the chick pens. The chicks chirped and huddled together. The room was warm and cozy, except for the man bashing his boot against the wall.

Thud!

Whack!

Thud!

"Gotcha," Frank McDonald yelled as he whacked an imaginary beetle.

Frank's eyes were glassy, his cheeks flushed, his movements alternating between smooth and jerky as he took a trip on the White Lightning train.

A mason jar of Barney's home brewed moonshine stood empty on the workbench beside him.

Frank's Blue Heeler stood in the doorway, tail tucked between his legs, whimpering. The dog didn't know what was wrong with its master but knew enough to be frightened.

Unable to stand it any longer, the dog bolted out of the half-open door and across the yard. He skidded to a stop on the porch and whined at the door until his master's wife let him in.

"What's wrong, Blue," Rainbow asked the agitated dog as he bolted through the doorway.

The German shepherd who had been sleeping peacefully by the woodstove raced in to see what was happening. The Blue Heeler whined and ran up to the shepherd, instinctively rolling onto its back in submission. The shepherd whined and nosed the other dog.

The heeler jumped up and paced anxiously around the room. After a few laps, the dog crawled under the kitchen table.

Rainbow bent down and looked at the dog, wondering what had spooked him. The shepherd joined her.

"It's okay, buddy. When you want to talk about it, I'm here for you," she crooned.

The heeler wagged its tail but wouldn't come out from under the table.

Rainbow shrugged and went back to work kneading the ball of dough on the kitchen counter. She hummed as she did so. The German shepherd went back to lie down by the warmth of the fire.

The door crashed open behind her.

Rainbow gasped and spun around.

The German shepherd scrambled to its feet. It dashed into the kitchen, barking and growling.

Rainbow silenced the dog with a hand signal and then lowered her flour speckled hand, palm flat, indicating that the dog should lie down. The dog responded instantly. The heeler whimpered under the table.

A man she barely recognized stood there, an axe in one hand, a hangman's noose in the other, bootless, and a bulging erection threatening to split his zipper open. His aura was an angry shade of red with black bullet like holes in it.

The shepherd bared its teeth.

"I've got it, honey, I know exactly how we're going to make this farm work," Rainbow's crazed husband said. "Forget the birds. Murder is where the money is. I've got it all worked out."

Frank spun on his heel, his muddy socks slipping on the polished floor, and headed back to the barn.

Rainbow dropped the dough on the counter, quickly wiped her hands, and grabbed her jacket.

"Come on, Blue," she croaked, her voice cracking. "You too, Bear. We're out'a here."

The dogs raced to her side, tails wagging furiously. They couldn't agree with her more.

Rainbow slipped on her flowered gumboots and peeked out the door. She saw Frank entering the barn, taking swings with the axe as if it was a baseball bat.

As soon as he disappeared inside the barn, she ran for the

front gate, slipped open the latch, and jogged down the road, heading for the one person she knew could help her – Betty Bruce.

The End... or is it?
Nope! Find out who dunnit in Book Three: *Murder Most Fowl*

If you enjoyed this novel, please consider leaving an honest review on Amazon. Just go to the bottom of the book's listing page and click on "Review this item".

Keep reading for a preview of the sequel – Book Three: *Murder Most Fowl.*

The Inspiration Behind The Book

SPOILER ALERT! DON'T READ UNTIL YOU'VE READ
THE DASTARDLY MR. DEEDS IN FULL

The cases of the severed feet that have washed up on the shores of various islands along the West Coast of British Columbia and Washington State has been well publicized. The real solution isn't quite as interesting as a zombie killing undertaker or a crooked funeral director, however, one case of fraud in the 'funeral business' provided the inspiration behind this story.

The FBI was involved in a bizarre crime: the owner of the Case Funeral Home was charged with desecrating a body after he cut the feet off a cadaver so that it would fit in a regular sized casket. The cadaver was over seven feet tall and the funeral homeowner was trying to save money.

For more information on the case of the severed feet in sneakers, here are some interesting links:

- https://en.wikipedia.org/wiki/Salish_Sea_human_foot_discoveries
- http://www.theprovince.com/quite+solved+mystery+severed+feet/10281333/story.html
- https://www.thisisinsider.com/british-columbia-find-severed-human-feet-on-shores-2019-2

and there are numerous more…check them out.

Murder Most Fowl - Preview

Murder Most Fowl Copyright

National Library of Canada Cataloguing in Publication Data
Hesse, Laura - 1959
Murder Most Fowl/by Laura Hesse
ISBN: 978-1999077402

Cover Design: Copyright 2019 Laura Hesse
Cover Artist: Autumn Sky, Self Pub Book Covers Inc.
Publisher: Running L. Productions, Vancouver Island, British Columbia, Canada

Distributed worldwide on Amazon

www.RunningLProductions.com

Prelude

Betty flew out of the bed. She quickly slipped a sweater over top of her pyjama top and a pair of blue jeans. She snatched up her cell phone and Summer River's ragged diary before racing down the stairs.

Outside the sun was setting behind Watchtower Mountain. Stars were beginning to sparkle over head. Creeping shadows danced among the evergreens that lined the driveway.

Betty felt chilled to the bone, despite the downy jacket and hiking boots she had slipped on before heading down to the Bristling Boar Pub.

Vi had no idea how much danger she was is, and neither did her father for that matter.

Betty increased her pace as she bolted down the hill, heading towards the landing. It got darker and darker as she ran down the gravel road until there was only starlight coupled with the muted glow from solar lanterns lining the odd driveway to light her way.

How on earth was she going to tell her father that she suspected his best friend of murder?

She tugged out her phone and breathlessly called Inspector Tom Powder, the lead investigator into the bizarre deaths of Summer River, Eliza Bone and Tiffany Hyde-White.

She slowed her pace briefly as her call to the Inspector went to voice mail.

"Tom, it's Betty," she huffed, breathless from her run. "I've been reading Summer's diary. I think I know who the father is. Call me as soon as you can."

Betty ended the call and increased her pace once again. Her

knees screamed from the beating they were taking. Her heart pounded against her rib cage. Sweat poured down her face and soaked her flannel PJ top beneath her sweater and coat. At fifty-two, she hadn't expected to be running a marathon, but she was glad she had kept up with her training, despite retiring from the force a few days ago.

***

At the same time that Betty was racing towards the pub, the beginning of North Shore Road, a hippie girl with flowing skirts, brightly colored gumboots, dread locked hair, and a homespun coat of many colors was racing towards Betty's house from her farm at the far end of North Shore Road. Her two dogs galloped along beside her.

Rainbow McDonald was fueled by terror. She ran as fast as her gumboots and skirts would allow. Her breath was a steamy cloud in front of her face. Her blue eyes were wild.

The German shepherd, a failed airport drug dog who hated crowds and loud noises, and a Blue Heeler, formerly man's best friend, ran along on either side of the frightened woman. They smelled the fear oozing off the woman in waves and kept pace, knowing instinctively that this wasn't the time to chase the myriad of rabbits and deer that scattered before them as they raced through the darkening night. It was in their nature to protect the pack and protect this woman they would, even if it cost them their lives.

Rainbow sprinted towards the one woman she knew could protect her from the madness that had taken over her husband: retired Sergeant Betty Bruce.

The sunset dwindled behind her and she found herself cursing the dark curtain of night that descended quickly upon them.

She flew past the moonshine maker's oceanfront home. There were lights on in the shed, but he scared her as much as her husband did right now, so she continued on.

Not long afterwards, she saw the moonlight glint off the metal gate that led up to Archie Bruce's house. She knew it well after spending a few days there communicating with Peaches, the poor Jersey cow that had been tasered by a trigger-happy cop, and Peaches buddy, Gertrude, a naughty pot-bellied pig who as always getting into trouble.

She had heard that Betty was living across the road from her father now.

"This way, Blue," she gasped, motioning for the Heeler to join her as she made an abrupt turn to the left, bumping into the shepherd. "Sorry, Bear."

She jogged up the winding drive. She sighed with relief when she saw that the lights were on in Betty's house on both floors.

She stomped up the steps to the front porch and then knocked on the door. No one answered. She tried to push the door open in case Betty was upstairs, but the door was locked.

Of course, she reasoned, Betty was used to living in the city and still had big city habits. She still found herself locking the door to their cabin at night, much to her husband's amusement.

She giggled hysterically, realizing she hadn't locked up the cabin when she left this time.

Rainbow circled the house.

She wiped the tears from her eyes and soldiered on.

An ear-piercing squeal and a baritone 'mooooo' met her from the barn. Gertrude raced out to greet her, Peaches following solemnly behind.

"Hey, Gertie, where's your mum," she asked the pot-bellied pig, the two dogs nosing forward cautiously.

Gertrude grunted in answer.

The German shepherd woofed; the Heeler whined.

"Bear, Blue, I'd like you to meet Gertrude and Peaches," Rainbow said, introducing her two dogs to the pot-bellied pig and Jersey cow.

"Gertrude, Peaches, this is Bear and Blue. I expect all of you to behave. No head butting the dogs, Gertie," she ordered the pig as the shepherd sniffed Gertrude's underbelly. Rainbow was relieved when the pig appeared to listen to her.

"And Peaches, no racing off. I won't allow Blue to chase you so ease up on the tension, little girl."

The cow walked forward, her hooves clicking on the cobble stone walkway in front of the barn. The cow and the Heeler met nose-to-nose. The cow bawled and the Heeler jumped backwards.

"Right, you all be good while I knock on the back door."

Rainbow climbed up onto the back porch and peeked through the patio door leading into the kitchen. There were no signs of movement inside. She knocked on the glass, but still there was no answer.

She bit her lip and paced back and forth, unsure of what to do.

Betty could be at her father's house or she could be at the pub. Rainbow didn't have any friends on the island so seeking out Betty and Archie Bruce were the only two choices she had. She liked Archie, but not his buddies. She balked at the idea of going to him for help in case one of them was there.

The other reason was that if Frank decided to look for her, he would immediately try Archie's place and she didn't want to be there if Betty wasn't there and her father was alone. She had seen Frank like this once before when he drank, but even then, the violence in his eyes as he held the axe in one hand and the rope noose in the other was over-the-top.

Rainbow tried opening the back door and patio door of Betty's house, but they were locked too.

Gertrude stood on stubby legs looking up at her. The pig grunted.

"What's that you say, Gert," Rainbow queried the pig.

The pig squealed, grunted and stomped one hoof. She then spun around and waddled back to the barn. Peaches licked her lip and followed her friend.

The dogs sat obediently, wagging their tails and waiting for instructions.

Rainbow wrapped her arms around her waist and shivered. She didn't know what to do but thought that Gertrude's offer to share the barn was the safest place for her and the dogs to go.

"Here, boys," she commanded the dogs.

The dogs instantly raced over and sat down beside her.

Rainbow rubbed their ears and under their chins.

"This way," she said, walking purposefully towards the barn. "We're going to take Gertrude up on her offer to stay the night with her."

She entered the small four stall barn and looked around. One stall was filled with hay and a second stall with dry sawdust and a few bales of straw. The other two stalls doors were open, the pig and cow having free rein to go wherever they wished.

Rainbow laughed. It felt good. It eased the tension in her back and shoulders.

Being a pet psychic had its advantages as well as its disadvantages. Being able to talk with Gertrude tonight made Rainbow feel much better. She knew that the pot-bellied pig and the two dogs would watch over her.

Rainbow entered Gertrude's stall. The pig had nestled down in a large bed of fresh straw. It looked warm and inviting. Rainbow snuggled in beside Gertrude, pulled her coat tightly around her slim body, and then patted her lap for the dogs to come in and join her.

Blue jumped at the chance to snuggle and leapt forward, his ears flopping. He plunked himself down in the straw beside Rainbow and then rested his head in her lap.

The German shepherd yawned and circled a couple of times in the doorway. He laid down, resting his head on his paws, facing outwards, on guard and ready to spring into action if needed.

***

Gertrude nosed the delightfully smelling woman she had invited to stay the night. The delicious scent of yeast, wheat and butter drifted off her coat and skin. That coupled with the pungent scent of sage intermingling with the sweet scents of honey and cinnamon made Gertrude's nose hairs quiver.

It was too bad the woman didn't have a dog biscuit in her pocket given that she had arrived with two foul scented dogs, but the pig was prepared to over look that given that she had helped Gertrude's best friend, Peaches, feel better. Despite the dogs, the woman was welcome to sleep in her bed at any time, whether it was here or across the road.

Gertrude and Peaches had just gotten home from the pub when Gertie heard her friend, Betty, race out of the house and down the driveway.

The pig supposed that she should have gone investigating or maybe should have run after Betty, but she was tired and no one at the pub except for her buddy, Reggie, had paid any attention to her head butts on the window.

What was a pig to do without a pint of draft to help keep her warm on a cold spring night except to go home to a warm bed of straw?

Gertie sighed and nuzzled the lovely new friend she had made. She may not have had a beer, but this was better than a pint anyway.

This concludes the preview of Book Three: *Murder Most Fowl*.
This book is the grand finale in the trilogy, but there is a stand alone fourth book for your enjoyment as well...
Book Four: *Gertrude & The Sorcerer's Gold*.

Follow Laura on her website @ www.RunningLProductions.com
to find out more about upcoming new releases
or join her on Goodreads or Bookbub.

Novels by Laura Hesse

The Holiday Series (family adventure):

One Frosty Christmas, The Great Pumpkin Ride, A Filly Called Easter, Independence and Valentino

Paranormal Thriller:

The Thin Line of Reason and Lucifer & Mary Jane: All The Devil's Horses

The Gumboot & Gumshoe Series:

Book One*: Gumboots, Gumshoes & Murder*
Book Two: *The Dastardly Mr. Deeds*
Book Three: *Murder Most Fowl*
Book Four*: Gertrude & The Sorcerer's Gold*
Book Five*: Chasing Santa*

The Silver Spurs Series

*The Silver Spurs Home for Aging Cowgirls
Bandits, Broads & Dirty Dawgs
Who Killed Cade*

Comedy & Adventure:

Peter Pan Wears Steel Toes

If you want to find hear about her upcoming releases, then visit her website at www.RunningLProductions.com.

About The Author

Laura Hesse

 Laura lives on Vancouver Island with two old cats and a rescue dog. When she's not writing, you'll find her kayaking or singing at a local jam.

She loves cozy mysteries and black comedies and finds inspiration in the strangest of places, but life is like that!

Peace and wellness to all.